GRIZZLY TALES

'CAUTIONARY TALES FOR LOVERS OF SQUEAM'

THE 'ME!' MONSTERS

DANGER

You are entering a cont

Do **NOT** open th

Which part of
'Do NOT open this book!'
do you NOT understand?

IS IT CAPITAL LETTERS YOU CAN'T READ?

Also in this series:

1 *Nasty Little Beasts*
2 *Gruesome Grown-ups*
3 *The 'Me' Monsters*
4 *Freaks of Nature*
5 *Terror Time Toys*
6 *Blubbers and Sicksters*

GRIZZLY TALES

'CAUTIONARY TALES FOR LOVERS' OF SQUEAM'

THE 'ME!' MONSTERS

JAMIE RIX

Illustrated by Steven Pattison

DANGER!

If you proceed beyond this point you will be exposed to high levels of selfishness and vanity that you may find worryingly attractive.

Orion
Children's Books

THE WICKED CHILDREN BEHIND THIS DOOR WILL TEACH YOU THINGS YOU DIDN'T OUGHT TO KNOW.

IF YOU LOVE YOUR PARENTS AND DON'T WANT TO MAKE THEM CROSS STAY OUT OF THE DARKNESS!

For Ben the BA

First published in Great Britain in 2007
by Orion Children's Books
a division of the Orion Publishing Group Ltd
Orion House
5 Upper St Martin's Lane
London WC2H 9EA

1 3 5 7 9 10 8 6 4 2

Printed in Great Britain

ISBN 978 1 84255 551 4

So you DON'T love your parents. This has been noted and your parents will be informed just before Christmas.

To help you survive in The Darkness we have designed an Anti-Contamination Suit that can be assembled from household objects.

All readers are required to wear this suit before proceeding.

ANTI-CONTAMINATION SUIT

Winter ear muffs to prevent unwanted intrusion or rude words

Dark glasses to cut down visibility when too scared to read on

Clothes pegs to eliminate any bad odours when you are thrown into the bowels of the earth

Net curtain to avoid bee stings *(Wrong suit. Sorry. Ed)*

Pillow Cases

Roman-style Duvet (10 toga)

Sharp pencil to prick pomposity and vain self-regard. Note book for recording your last words. Freshen-up towelettes to mop beads of perspiration from top lip. Mobile phone to call for help. Hammer to beat off The Dark Elves of Mordor. Lipstick to bribe The Pink Witches of L'Oreal

Oven gloves for shaking hands with the Devil

Discreet towel to avoid accidents when reader experiences moments of gut wrenching fear

Pillow Cases

Wellington boots for wading through the filthy little minds of children

WELCOME TO
THE HOTHELL DARKNESS
BREAKFAST 7.30AM - 9.30AM.

DO YOU FEEL LUCKY? FOR TODAY AND TODAY ONLY WE HAVE A VERY SPECIAL PROMOTION HERE IN THE HOTHELL DARKNESS. STAY FOR JUST ONE NIGHT AND GET THE REST OF ETERNITY FREE! YES COMPLETELY FREE UNTIL THE END OF TIME! WOW! IT'S WHAT WE LIKE TO CALL OUR SOMETHING FOR NOTHING DEAL. YOU DO NOTHING AND WE GET SOMETHING IN RETURN. NAMELY YOU. SO HURRY DOWN TO THE FRONT DESK NOW TO FILL OUT YOUR REGISTRATION CARD AND SEAL YOUR FATE FOR EVER!

The Night-night Porter

REMEMBER ANACONDA BUNGEE JUMPS CAN GO UP AS WELL AS DOWN AT THE DISCRETION OF THE MANAGEMENT. PERSONAL BELONGINGS CAN BE LOST WITHOUT PRIOR NOTICE. BEDS CAN BE BURNT IF WE FEEL LIKE A BONFIRE. AND LAUGHING AT PERSONAL PHOTOGRAPHS UNTIL YOU CRY IS OBLIGATORY BEHAVIOUR FOR ALL STAFF. FOOD IS NOT INCLUDED (NOT THAT YOU'LL NEED ANY WHEN WE USE YOUR STOMACH FOR THE INTER-DORMITORY BASKETBALL MATCH!)

I can't keep you away, can I?

You'll be glad to hear that things have changed since you were here last. They had to. I was losing too many guests. Not to food poisoning, bed bugs or accidents in the kitchen – like that poor girl Brenda who fell into the in-SINK-erator and made such a mess of my Venetian splash-back tiles – but to GENUINE misunderstandings.

It would appear that some of my guests were SCARED of ME! I can't think why.

Was it the fact that I hide millipedes in my beard or dry my hands on the backs of children's hair?

Was it was the cane I swish when I patrol the corridor or the severed fingers I leave sticking out of wall plugs to warn children of the dangers of electricity?

Was it was my love of maggots in muesli for breakfast or the funny little way I have of clearing my throat onto guests' scrambled eggs?

If it was any of these. I apologise. There. I've said it.

Now that you have no more reason to fear me. you can have no more reason not to stay. That's settled then.

Your room's still ready.

Shall we do our little test to see how BAD you really are? I wouldn't want anyone sampling the inhospitality of the Hothell Darkness without being really sure that they deserved it.

ANSWER TRUTHFULLY

When you pass a mirror do you glance casually at your reflection or hug up for a bit of self-snogging?

1. Would you like my last Rolo? (Of course you would, you pig. You've had all the rest.)

2. If a person has twelve apples, a melon, four peaches, two grapefruit and eighteen oranges in one hand; and one side of beef, fourteen yoghurts, a bottle of squash, twelve loo rolls, three cartons of ice cream, two packets of chocolate fingers, six bags of crisps, twenty-one potatoes and a carton of chocolate milk in the other, why aren't you helping them carry the shopping?

3. Who ate all the pies?

If your answers are 'Yes', 'Yes', 'Don't Know' and 'Me!' you are a 'Me!' Monster and are well bad enough to stay in this hothell. If your answers vary in any way at all, you can stay too, because I've locked the front door now and put the key in my underpants. OK?

Just in case you were thinking of trying to steal the keys back, you should know this; I haven't changed my underpants in years. That's why I crunch when I walk.

If you want something to do while you're slowly rotting in your room, you could always read our Visitor's Book. It contains the stories of some of our other guests, which is why I call it The Book of Grizzly Tales — because they are not nice stories. Oh, dear me, no! They're horrible. The children in these stories are all Me! Monsters, which means they only think about themselves.

Me! Me! Me! Me! Me! Me! Me! Me! Me! Me! Me! Me!
There's one of them shouting now, because the bath oil's too hot (it doesn't work if it's not boiling).

Me! Me! Me! Me! Me! Me! Me! Me! Me! Me! Me! Me!
And there's the rest of them. That's the trouble with Me! Monsters, they all sound the same.

Ribbet Ribbet! Splat!

Except for that one. That guest came to a particularly sticky end, unlike this first tale which comes from a particularly sticky beginning.

Read the following essay and see if you can make sense of it.

my name is bs brogan i was born under the mark of the broken typewriter a 1925 frontstroke maskelyne grasshopper in a basement room underneath the typewriter repair shop where my grandfather worked for fifty years i was a normal looking child with a shock of black hair and toes that pointed inwards like a question mark the doctors bound them with splints until they grew straight i crawled when i was one and walked when i was two but i didnt speak until i was six my silence caused my parents much worry the doctors ran tests on me to see if i was deaf or dumb but i was neither i did not want to speak and therefore i did not but then i did and everything i had never said rushed out of my mouth like a waterfall and when i try to write it down it comes out of my pen so fast that this is how it looks no time to stop no time to pause just words and words jostling for position on the page facts and thoughts and truths competing for space silly facts like when im not at school or home i live in batty wood where goblins keep the man in the moon awake by grinding their teeth my mummy was a beauty queen and my daddy plays dominoes on saturday night with a horse called fiddle at least i think its a horse and i think its names fiddle because it cant speak and has never actually told me to my face talking of which i have got a little nose brown eyes and teeth in my mouth that im sure once belonged to ann boleyn one of henry the eighths dead wives who had her head cut off and teeth put into a jar of beetroot pickle which is where i found them

This essay. entitled 'A Short History Of Me'. was written by a nine-year-old boy. His name. as you've probably guessed. was B.S. Brogan and he had a short but rather noisy life.

The Night-flight Porter

THE APOSTROPHIC EXPOSITOR

Having wilfully remained silent for the first six years of his life, when he did finally speak, words poured out of B.S. Brogan in a torrent of gobbledygook.

Typical Me! Monster

His grandfather did *not* own a typewriter shop and had never mended a 1925 model of a Frontstroke Maskelyne Grasshopper typewriter. It's true that his feet were bent inwards at birth like a question mark, as if his body was questioning its own existence, but he had never played in Batty Wood, the Man in the Moon had not complained about noisy goblins, and if his father had ever played dominoes with a horse he'd kept it a closely guarded secret. As for the teeth; he had seen a pair of wooden teeth in the Tower of London when he was three, but they weren't Ann Boleyn's and he certainly didn't find them in a jar of beetroot pickle. They had belonged to a strange, blue-eyed monk who had stopped in front of his pushchair outside the Bloody Tower and smiled knowingly revealing a mouthful of uneven brown teeth. B.S. Brogan had always remembered the monk, because of his shock of bleached blond hair.

Once he had started to speak, B.S Brogan made up for six years of self-imposed silence by talking non-stop. It was as if he had never heard anything quite so beautiful as the sound of his own voice. The day after the words arrived his worried parents rushed into the doctor for a check up.

'And your name is?' said the doctor.

my name is bs brogan hello are you a doctor a medical doctor i mean not a doctor of philosophy because i wouldnt ask a doctor of philosophy what was wrong with me unless i had a problem with my soul not my shoe sole my eternal soul talking of eternal its a new perfume for girls and boys i think although ive never met a boy who wears perfume not a nice smelling perfume ive met plenty of boys who wear natural perfume and stink is that a stethoscope round your neck that word sounds like bathyscaphe which is what men dive to the bottom of the ocean in but why would a doctor need one of those unless you wanted to dive into my blood and look for a giant squid

This splurge of nonsense would have continued all day had the doctor not stopped it by inserting a lollipop into B.S. Brogan's gob.

'My goodness,' he exclaimed, as the noise was plugged, 'he *does* like to talk, doesn't he?'

'He doesn't know when to stop,' said his mother.

'His constant drivel is driving us nuts,' added his father. 'Is there nothing you can do?'

'Nothing at all,' said the doctor. 'It has to get worse before it gets better!'

This perked up B.S. Brogan's mother no end. 'So it *will* get better?'

'Oh yes,' said the doctor, 'when he dies. I don't think you've fully grasped what's happened. In those early years when he refused to speak his brain was filling up with the words he wasn't using. It swelled and swelled until eventually it exploded!'

'His brain has exploded?' gasped his mother.

'Like a huge roaring river bursting its banks,' laughed the doctor. 'All those words are just swimming around inside his head like dead cows on a flood plain.'

* * *

For the next three years, the blather-fest of bilge that poured from their son's mouth drove Mr and Mrs Brogan crazy. It was like living with a steam train in the sitting room; chatterbox, chatterbox, chatterbox choo . . .

The noise went on day and night, depriving not just B.S. Brogan's parents of sleep, but their neighbours too. Before long people started moving out of the area. Even the rats relocated to a sewer in Birmingham.

Then one Tuesday morning, when B.S. Brogan was nine, Mrs Brogan suddenly slapped her hands over her ears and screamed, 'STOP!!'

Sensing that his wife had reached the end of her tether Mr Brogan suggested a trip to the zoo, hoping that being outdoors might lessen the noise. All it did was lessen the population of the zoo. By lunchtime, B.S. Brogan's witless chatter had bored the mynah birds to death, caused three Japanese snapping turtles to commit harikari on their sunning stone and reduced the number of lemmings in the world by three hundred and fifty thousand.

'My, that went well,' mocked Mrs Brogan after the family had been escorted off the premises.

no it did not said B.S. Brogan if you hadnt scared all the animals to death with your miserable face they might have let us stay

* * *

With nine came a new problem. The words still poured out of his mouth, but now when he didn't have anything nice to say B.S. Brogan would say something nasty.

At school, nobody wanted to sit next to him. This was not just because he talked through every lesson, but also because his rudeness meant that the teacher always had her eye on him.

kumquats are delicious if you marinade them in milk and sprinkle a sprig of rosemary on top i got that from a recipe book im writing called milky kumquat recipes by bs brogan thats me you see but you probably knew that already because theres a big clue every morning when our form teacher miss tiddlypush her at the front with the fat arms and big black moustache like a mexican footballer takes the register im the boy who puts up his hand when she calls out the name bs brogan

'What did you just say?!' gasped Miss Tiddlypush, hiding her top lip with the board wipe. 'I do NOT have a big black moustache like a Mexican footballer!' She moved him into a desk on his own, but it made no difference. He carried on chatting whether people were listening or not.

when i was seven i had a monkey with a big black moustache it was a chinchilla called caroline which is an incredible coincidence because miss tiddlypush is called caroline too as well as looking like a monkey with a beard oh look everyone thats gross that new girl fatimahs picking her nose ugh save some room for lunch fatimah

When Fatimah cried B.S. Brogan was moved into the corridor outside the headmistress's office where he carried on talking to the wall. From there he was moved into the office itself, where the headmistress gave him a talking-to. Unfortunately *her* talking to was not as loud or as long as the talking-to that B.S. Brogan gave *her*, and four hours later he emerged from her office the victor.

When the headmistress resigned, citing as her reason 'exhaustion from listening to B.S. Brogan's tripe-talk', the school governors decided that B.S. Brogan had a nasty case Me-At-The-Centre-of-The-Universe syndrome which manifested itself in verbal diarrhoea and a fear of listening to anyone else's voice. They asked the School Nurse to cure him, but after four days of treatment, she was baffled.

'I can find no explanation for this boy's extraordinary ability to breathe in and keep talking at the same time,' she told the governors, 'other than this – he's a fish. He's got gills behind his ears to let the air in.'

But no gills were found. In despair, the teachers resorted to gags; thick strips of calico wound around B.S. Brogan's mouth and secured with gaffer

tape to prevent his tongue from moving, but the European Court of Human Rights had a couple of words to say about that and the gags were banned.

Those judges at the European Court of Human Rights are a bunch of interfering busybodies. Only last week they tried to close this hothell down for misuse of an 'in-sink-erator'. Can you believe it? I was the victim. That crooked plumber charged me £300 to get those severed toes out.

* * *

Matters spiralled even further out of control. Unable to learn with B.S. Brogan chatting in the class children were taken out of the school by their parents until B.S. Brogan was the only pupil left. With nobody to teach, the teachers jumped ship too until there was just one of them left. She was an old-fashioned lady called Miss Syntax, from the learning-by-rote school of English grammar. She also happened to be deaf. This deafness meant that she was completely unaffected by his barrage of nasty names and nonsensical twittering. It should have been a marriage made in Heaven, but it wasn't. She may not have been able to hear, but Miss Syntax could *see* perfectly well and what she saw when she looked at B.S. Brogan's written work shocked her to the core. B.S. Brogan wrote as he talked, without pause or hesitation.

'No!' she cried when she first set eyes on 'A Short History of Me'. 'This is not acceptable. If you don't use punctuation how are you ever going to make yourself understood?'

B.S. Brogan caught his breath. **by texting** he said. And with that one cheeky remark, Miss Syntax threw in the towel and the school closed down.

* * *

It was a black day for Mr and Mrs Brogan. Word of their son's loose tongue had spread fast and there was not a school in the country prepared to take him on. This meant that Mr and Mrs Brogan had to educate him at home, but with only one GCSE and a diploma in Forecourt Management between them neither felt qualified to do so. They advertised for a home teacher in *ASBO Kids Weekly*, a magazine that catered for disruptive pupils who had been excluded from school. A week later they received a reply from an English teacher who called himself the Apostrophic Expositor and claimed to teach the Grammar of the Eternal Pause. His letter came with a glowing reference from his previous employers.

To Whom It May Concern
In so far as brevity is a virtue, use him.

Rob Dawnn

Mr and Mrs Brogan were intrigued and wrote back asking him to start on Monday.

* * *

The Apostrophic Expositor arrived with all his worldly belongings at 6.00 am. He was a tall man dressed in the shapeless brown habit of a monk and carried in his hands a small wooden bowl, a tin mug and a large leather book edged in gold. He removed his hood to reveal eyes of blue and a shock of dyed blond hair.

'You must be B.S. Brogan's new teacher,' beamed Mr Brogan. 'Do come in. My son's still in bed.'

'Are you hungry?' asked Mrs Brogan. 'Would you like some breakfast?'

The stranger did not reply. He simply stood in the hall and waited.

Mr and Mrs Brogan were unsure what he wanted from them. 'Can you speak?' Mr Brogan asked tentatively.

'I do speak,' he whispered, 'but I say things only once, therefore I must choose my words carefully.'

'I see.' Mr Brogan coughed lightly. 'Perhaps you could explain what is meant by the Grammar of the Eternal Pause?'

'When you pause eternally you are dead and when you are dead you are silent,' said the monk, sitting down on the carpet in front of the door. 'I believe that silence is a virtue. Here shall I await my pupil's arrival. His lesson shall start the moment he arrives.'

'Is there anything we can bring you while you are waiting?' asked Mrs Brogan. The Apostrophic Expositor held out his tin mug. 'Some cold water,' he said, 'a sheet of white paper and a pencil.'

* * *

Fifteen minutes later, B.S. Brogan arrived downstairs in a flurry of withering words.

i was told you were the only teacher in the world who could teach me but they didnt tell me that you had hair the colour of dog sick if i gave you something to unlock a door do you know what that would make you ill give you a clue its got a red bottom i bet youve got a red bottom from being rubbed all the time by that itchy potato sack thing youre wearing do you give up youd be a monkey a monk key dont smile if you dont want to theres no law that says you have to have a sense of humour but you should be careful because people might think youre a chicken because chickens dont smile either and they might accidentally wring your neck dont i know you from somewhere your brown teeth ring a bell phwaaaaaw someones dropped a ripe one ding dong dell who made that smell binky bonky binky whoever did is stinky i bet its you sneaking one out through your potato sack because you look like a dirty old tram

He would have continued forever had the Apostrophic Expositor not held up his hand in the

shape of a swan's beak and closed it, by touching the tip of his thumb with the tip of his middle finger. B.S. Brogan closed his mouth as he did so and for the first time in three and a half years stopped talking.

'B.S. Brogan,' said the monk. 'You have come to a crossroads. One path leads to a life worth living the other to a future that is *no* future. For the sake of world peace you must learn when to stop. If you never draw a breath you will never make sense. You must breathe or you will suffocate with words. Pause or *be* paused. Let us begin our first lesson.' The boy blinked as if caught in a trance, then sat down opposite the ascetic, who pushed the pencil and paper across the floor towards him. 'Punctuate this sentence, then write it out one hundred times,' he said. B.S. Brogan picked up the piece of paper and stared at what the monk had written.

That that is is that that is not
is not is not that it it is

Then he screwed up the piece of paper and threw it over his shoulder.

no he said go shove your head in a beetroot boiler who needs grammar anyway only fussy old women like you in your baggy brown dress with nothing better to do than stick your nose in where its not wanted i dont do punctuation it stops the words and the words must flow

'If you can't say something nice,' whispered the Apostrophic Expositor, 'best say nothing at all.'

are you threatening me bristled the boy are you trying to tell me what i can and cant say

'I'm   warning   you,'   said   the   monk.

the only time ive ever been scared in my life was when i had a sore throat and thought i was going to lose my voice but youre just a teacher and teachers dont scare me if a teacher has nobody to teach theyre not a teacher so im the powerful one out of the two of us because if you dont have me as your pupil you dont exist

'Then so be it,' murmured the Apostrophic Expositor. 'You have chosen unwisely. As you will not learn to punctuate for yourself, I shall have to punctuate YOU. We shall read this book instead.' He placed his leather book on the carpet. From the outside, it looked like an illuminated manuscript that a mediaeval monk might have devoted his life to inscribing, but when the thoroughly modern monk opened the front cover the pages were blank.

you are mad snorted B.S. Brogan i knew you were how can i read something that isnt there

'Just say the first thing that comes into your head,' said the monk. 'It shouldn't be hard. After all it's what you've been doing for the last three and a half years!'

ok said B.S. Brogan ok and he lined up the nastiest thing he could think of saying. The words in his head were: 'i dont need punctuation its boring and pointless im never going to use it in the whole of my life so leave me alone or ill kick you up the colon'

But the words that came out were quite different, as if an unseen hand was dragging them from his mouth. The words that he actually uttered were, 'These are the Last Words of B.S. Brogan. I want them to be written down as a deterrent to other chatty children who don't know when to stop.' Saying them pulled him up short. 'That's not right,' he faltered. 'That wasn't what I wanted to say.'

'The choice is no longer yours,' smiled the Apostrophic Expositor. 'From now on the book is in charge of your words. Behold.' The book had sucked in B.S. Brogan's words and arranged them at the top of the first page.

'But they're punctuated!' he cried.

'All the better for understanding,' said the monk.

'Now hang on a minute!' yelled the boy. 'I thought Last Words were for people who were going to die.'

'We're all going to die,' smiled the monk, flashing his wooden teeth. 'Some of us sooner than others.'

A monk after my own heart!

'In that case I don't want to these to be my Last Words!' yelled the boy.

'Nobody ever does,' said the monk as B.S. Brogan's second, third and fourth sentences appeared on the page alongside the first.

* * *

For three days the book filled up with B.S. Brogan's Last Words. As he protested against the monk's evil magic, as he wailed for this cruel torture to stop, as he begged to regain control of his tongue, the book recorded it all. It extracted the words from his head and rearranged them into clear sentences on the page. When he tired and his eyelids closed the monk woke him up by splashing him with cold water from his mug. On the morning of the fourth day the flow of words started to taper off. By tea time B.S. Brogan had so little left to say that he was taking breaths between sentences, pausing to allow the meaning of his words to come out. But by

then it was too late, for by then B.S. Brogan had run out of words. He didn't yet know it, but inside his head there were only two words left.

'The End' he announced suddenly, taking himself by surprise.

Then there was silence.

'Is that his punishment?' Mr and Mrs Brogan asked when the Apostrophic Expositor fetched them into the hall to see the positive change in their son. 'Is he to be mute for the rest of his life?'

'Not at all,' said the monk. 'I shall make far better use of him than that.' As he kissed the cover of the book, B.S. Brogan felt a sharp pain in his stomach. Seconds later, his bellybutton blew out like a champagne cork. Through the raw, ragged hole his intestines exploded into the hall. Mile after mile of red gore unravelled from inside him. His body collapsed as its stuffing was extracted. It shrivelled and turned inside out as his legs, chest, hands and arms were sucked into the book, until all that was left was a tiny, round, black-haired head. Then even that was gone; sucked onto the page; stuck permanently to the paper just after the 'd' of 'End'.

B.S. Brogan's life had literally come to a full stop.

As the old saying goes: *That that is, is. That that is not, is not. Is that not it? It is.*

And that that is *not* is B.S. Brogan!

I'll let you into a little secret. I've got him down here now. When I asked the monk if he'd transfer B.S. Brogan into The Darkness. he was only too glad to get rid of him. He arrived yesterday in a letter. so I'm using him now for the first time. That was B.S. Brogan there. Did you spot him? He's the only full stop on this page who gives it TOO MUCH LIP!

Tell you what. let's play a game. I love games . . . so long as I win. I'll hide B.S. Brogan somewhere in this book and you have to find him. It'll be a bit like 'Where's Wally?' without Wally. The person who finds B.S. Brogan will win a free luxury WEEKEND in The Hothell Darkness DUNGEON. plus an exclusive Hothell Darkness TOWELLING ROBE. Made from the finest bat skin. it comes

complete with in-built cuff-manacles for speedy attachment to wall cleats and extra deep pockets for carrying your ball and chain!

Post entries to;

'*Where's B.S. Brogan?*' *Competition*
Long Stay Bookings Manager
The Hothell Darkness

To prove I love games I'm going to tell you how to play my version of Postman's Knock. It's a lot more sophisticated than the boring version where a girl and a boy eat a strand of spaghetti until they kiss. For my game you need a postman, a spade, a shallow grave and a lot of patience. Sometimes you can be waiting literally HOURS for the post to arrive. Then when the POSTMAN KNOCKS (hence the name of the game) you open the door, bash him on the head with a spade, dump him in the shallow grave and say,

'Right. Are you going to stop delivering junk mail or not?!' and if he says 'no' or nothing at all, because you've hit him a bit too hard with the spade, you cover him up and plant grass seed on his grave so that the police can't find him.

It's a great game for parties. The worms like it too.

I know a girl who'd like to play Postman's Knock. Not my version (sadly) but the sissy kissing one. It's fair to say that this girl likes kissing more than is good for her!

KISS AND MAKE-UP

At one particular school, in one particular playground, there is one particular spot where one particular girl stands in any particular weather. Her name is Holly Hotlips. Every day she stands beneath the boughs of The Kissing Tree, under a sign that says 'FREE KISSES HERE!' and puckers her lips in readiness for a snog. But the snog never comes, because snogging is something only *two* people can do, and the boys at this particular school did not want to snog Holly.

'Why not?' she wailed one Tuesday lunchtime, as the two hundredth boy that day walked past her with his nose in the air. 'What's wrong with me?'

'You're a bit desperate,' said an honest lad called Harold Seagoon. 'No offence, but a kiss is not a kiss unless you do it with someone you like.'

'You mean, you don't like me!' howled Holly.

'I don't *know* you,' he said.

Holly gulped back the tears and stepped forward. 'How do you do?' she said, firmly shaking Harold's hand. 'You know me now, so how about it?'

'Tempting,' laughed Harold, 'but you're far too young to be kissed.'

This thought had never crossed Holly's mind. Then later that night, whilst combing her hair before bed, her reflection said much the same thing. 'You know what your problem is,' it said.

'I've gone mad?' gasped Holly. 'When did you start talking?'

'Ever since you started listening,' said the cunning reflection. 'The secret to getting a kiss is *looking* older.'

'*Looking* older,' said Holly. 'Gosh! I didn't know that.'

'Of course you didn't,' said her reflection. 'That's why it's a secret.' And it went on to explain why boys only liked kissing girls who were twice their age.

This is rubbish of course, but Holly didn't know that. A reflection only says what its creator wants to hear, which is why you should never trust one. It's a vain, insubstantial thing, just as much a Me! Monster as the person looking in the mirror, and as such is best ignored. But Holly Hotlips was a silly girl who thought that kissing boys was the most important thing in the world.

> Such pish and tosh deserves everything it gets
> . . . which, thankfully, it DID!

Egged on by her reflection, the muddle-headed girl made a wish.

'I wish . . . I wish . . . I wish I looked older,' she cried. Then she jumped into bed and waited for her wish to come true.

* * *

Two hours later she was woken by a rat-a-tat-tat on the bridge of her nose. Her eyes sprang open. Through a sleepy haze she saw a creature hovering above her. It appeared to be about six inches tall, to be glowing pinky-white like mother of pearl, and to have something fluttery behind its back.

'Are you a fairy?' yawned Holly, still struggling to wake up. 'Are you real or part of a dream?'

'I'm real, darlink,' it said in a husky female voice that dripped with honey and gravel. 'You want to age and look a dish, so here I am to grant your wish!'

Holly scrunched up her eyes then opened them again. This time the fog had cleared and she could see the creature in all its beauty. It was indeed a fairy, as striking as a 1950s film star. She had a powdered face, long luscious lashes, ruby red lips and wavy blond hair that flicked and curled around her face like tumbling vine leaves.

'You've come to make me older,' smiled Holly when she realized what was happening. 'Pleasure to meet you!'

'I wish it was,' said the fairy. 'What you see is not the whole story, I'm afraid. There's somebody I need to warn you about.'

Before she had finished her sentence, the fairy's head swivelled. Her face whizzed around like a spinning top and came to rest on the back of her head. Only the back of her head wasn't quite as Holly was expecting. Instead of hair there was a large, unfriendly face with bulbous eyes, a crooked nose and a long thin chin covered in grey whiskers. Its cheeks and eyelids were peppered with clusters of tiny warts and right in the middle of its forehead, looking like a third eye, was a large, black verruca.

'Does she mean me?' it cackled, as the head span back to the pretty face.

'Go away!' she ordered her ugly other half.

'Gosh!' gasped Holly. 'You've got eyes in the back of your head.'

'And ears and cheeks,' sighed the film star fairy, 'and a hairy nose as well! You see, I'm called—' The head whipped round so that the ugly face could interrupt.

'*We're* called!' it snapped, before spinning off again.

'Sorry,' said the pretty face. '*We're* called the Two-Faced Fairy, dear, for rather obvious reasons.'

'Yes,' said Holly. 'I think I can guess.'

'I'm the good fairy.'

'And I'm the bad!' growled the unsightly face, taking over once again. 'Well, who wouldn't be bad, looking backwards all the time?'

'Why?' asked Holly.

'Because I've got nothing to look forward to!' screamed the bad fairy as the tug of war started again.

'Oh, do stop butting in!' shouted the good fairy.

'It's not me with a face like a butt,' howled the bad fairy, losing her face almost immediately to her painted sister.

'She is so vulgar,' said the pretty one. 'I'd better get on before she corrupts you for ever. Now, Holly, darlink, you wish to look older to get kissed. Nothing could be simpler. My advice is wear lots of make-up.'

'My advice,' shrieked the ugly face, 'is grab him by the hair and snog him till his lips turn blue.'

'I'll go with the make-up,' said Holly sensibly.

Blue lips were for whales.

'Very wise, dear,' said the good fairy. Then she waved her magic wand and a bundle of make-up materialized and fell onto her bed. 'Now should you need me again write "HELP!" on your window with a lipstick and I shall be by your side in the twinkle of a glitter wand!' Holly was so happy that she leant forward to give the good fairy a kiss, but just as she did so, the bad fairy span herself around and puckered up right in front of Holly's eyes. Holly screamed and backed away. The bad fairy's lips were so dry and wrinkled it was like kissing a cat's bottom!

Ribbet Ribbet! Splat!

Sounds like one of the 'Me!' Monsters has got a frog in his throat!

* * *

The next day was Wednesday and for the first time in her life Holly wore make-up to school. Being a novice, however, she wasn't very good at putting it on. Her face was orange, her cheeks were red, her eyebrows were blue and her pink mouth was smeared from one ear to the other. She looked ridiculous, but Holly wasn't bothered, because Holly thought she looked older. The fact that she scared small children on her way to school, and newborn babies leaped from their prams with cries of 'Agh! It's a monster!' did not lessen her self-confidence. The fact that when she knelt down to tie up her shoelace a greengrocer tried to polish her face and pop it in a box of tangerines did nothing to dent Holly's belief in her own gorgeousness. She gazed at herself in shop windows and fell in love with how she looked.

'I look at least sixteen!' she purred. 'Perfect for kissing.'

At break, however, the sad truth was told when she stood under the Kissing Tree and waited for her first snog.

Instead of luscious lip action, the boys simply screamed and ran away. 'I'm not kissing Mr Punch!' cried one.

'And I'm not kissing a freaky clown!' shouted another.

'Come back!' she yelled. 'Don't I look older?'

The playground fell silent with embarrassment. Who was going to tell her? A snotty junior was the only one brave enough to broach the truth.

'With that polished orange head of yours,' he said, 'you look like a conker.'

Holly Hotlips cried through the rest of break, through late morning lessons, through lunch, through afternoon lessons, through supper, telly and bath, until finally she had to stop before she fainted from dehydration. Before she went to bed she wrote 'HELP!' on her bedroom window and waited for the Two-Faced Fairy to come.

* * *

'It's obvious what went wrong,' said the good fairy, five minutes later. 'You weren't wearing enough make-up.'

'Is that why the boys wouldn't kiss me?' gasped Holly.

'Absolutely, darlink!'

'So it's nothing to do with me being unattractive?'

'Of course not,' pooh-poohed the good fairy. 'The more make-up you wear the older you look.'

'I'm wearing loads!' screeched the bad fairy, swivelling into view.

'Why are you so bad?' asked Holly all of a sudden.

'Why are *you* so stupid?'

'I'm not stupid!'

'Then why do you cry all day when the boys won't kiss you?' The head revolved swiftly.

'That's quite enough poison from you,' snapped the good fairy, only to find herself losing face again.

'I can't help being bad,' howled her dark side. 'Ever since a troll stole my face and gave me his instead I've been in a bad mood! You think I like this ugly old mug? I'd give anything to change it!'

'Don't get her started,' said the good fairy. 'Now we're here is to make you look older, so . . .'

'*I'm* not!' shrieked the bad fairy. 'The reason I'm here is to get a new face.' The spinning head was starting to make Holly feel dizzy.

'So here's what we're going to do,' trilled the good fairy, conjuring up another ton of make-up from thin air. 'Pop that lot on tomorrow and I guarantee you'll be fighting the boys off!' Then with a push and a shove and a puff of pink smoke the Two-Faced Fairy was gone.

* * *

The next morning Holly rose early and sat in front of the bathroom mirror applying her make-up. She used oodles of foundation, lashings of mascara, rubbings of rouge and nearly three tubes of lipstick. When she had finished, she left the room, only to re-enter it seconds later with the intention of catching herself unawares. She glanced at herself in the mirror and gasped as if greeting an old (and very beautiful) friend. 'Oh hi,' she chuckled. 'No, let me guess. You're twenty-two.'

It still didn't work. At school, the boys took one look at the multi-coloured mask on top of Holly's neck and dubbed her 'Puke-Face'. Then they ran away.

'But I look older!' she protested as she fought back the tears.

'You look ugly like a horrid old troll.' It was the snotty Junior again. He didn't know it, but a truer word had never been said.

Being told that she looked like a horrid old troll brought Holly to her senses. She realized that she had been made to look stupid by her reflection. She didn't need to look older to get a kiss. She didn't need to wear make-up. She just needed to be Holly, and if a kiss was meant to happen it would happen, in its own time.

'I wish I didn't have any make-up on at all!' she cried. And when she got home her wish had been granted. There was a note on her bed.

> Dear Holly,
> Sorry make-up didnt work. Even good fairies can get it wrong! Please accept this free pot of Vanishing Cream to make up for my mistake. Use it to take your face off.
> Love and wishes,
> # The Good Fairy
> PS Good luck with the snogging!

'What a good fairy she is,' thought Holly, unscrewing the lid from the jar of Vanishing Cream. Then she gently rubbed the cool white lotion into her face and removed all traces of the hated make-up that had made her look so ridiculous.

But when she woke on Friday morning, Holly Hotlips received the shock of her short and shallow life. When she looked in the bathroom mirror *nothing* looked back. Apart from her ears, the Vanishing Cream had made her face vanish!

'What Vanishing Cream?' said the good fairy, responding to another cry for 'HELP!' 'I didn't give you any Vanishing Cream.'

'But it was here on my bed,' sobbed the faceless girl, 'with this note.'

'Wait a minute,' said the good fairy. 'I know who's responsible for this. Come out here this instant!' she yelled, but the bad fairy wasn't putting in an appearance just to be shouted at. She stayed tucked up in the good fairy's hair. '*You* did this, didn't you?'

'Might have done,' came the muffled reply.

'But how was I supposed to know it wasn't from you?' wailed Holly.

'Because I'm "good" and don't use words like "snogging"!' said the good fairy. 'It's a horrid word.'

'It's not as bad as "tongue sandwich"!' giggled the bad fairy, 'or "tonsil hockey"!'

'Be quiet!' shouted Holly. 'Thanks to your evil trick I haven't got a face!'

'No,' sniggered the bad fairy, 'but I have!' Then with a whoop of joy she revealed her makeover in all its glory. Gone was the blobby face of the ugly troll, and in its place was a new pretty face. Holly's!

Of course Holly couldn't see it, because she didn't have any eyes, but she *did* have ears, which meant that when the good fairy reassured Holly that getting a new face couldn't be simpler, Holly heard every word.

'Just paint one on with make-up!' said the good-fairy, smugly.

'Oh shut up and give me back my real face!' yelled Holly. But as she lunged into the darkness to catch her tormentor, the two-faced fairy skipped out of her reach, blew a raspberry in her ear and with a tasteless laugh of triumph vanished into the ether.

Holly never saw her face or indeed the two-faced fairy again. With neither mouth nor lips, kissing became impossible for her. She stopped standing under the Kissing Tree, gave up trying to be snogged and settled for the life of a child instead.

'I want to grow up when I'm ready,' she told her parents and teachers.

And nobody disagreed with her.

I'm delighted to say that Holly lives down here now and is deeply unhappy. I don't know why, because she's very popular with the other children. It's her blank face, I think. They pin her down on the kitchen floor and play POTATO FACE with her. It's a right laugh. They stick different vegetables on the front of her head to give her funny faces a strawberry nose, carrot lips, turnip eyes. The other day they gave her SLUG eyebrows. They stuck the slugs on with cocktail sticks and they wiggled up and down all night. She looked like a ventriloquist's dummy. It was brilliant.

I nearly forgot . . .

A WORD OF WARNING

WATCH OUT FOR THE TWO-FACED FAIRY. I'VE GOT ANOTHER CHILD DOWN HERE WHO FELL FOR HER CHARMS. PASTY DOUGHBALL OF A BOY CALLED HAMISH, WHO BELIEVED HER WHEN SHE SAID SHE WAS GOING TO TURN HIM INTO THE MOST HANDSOME BOY IN THE WORLD. HE WAS SO VAIN HE GAVE HER EVERYTHING SHE WANTED. ALL HIS HAIR PRODUCTS, FACE CREAM, MOISTURISER AND PERFUME. TURNED OUT SHE MEANT HANSOM, AS IN HANSOM CAB! NOT QUITE WHAT HE HAD IN MIND, SPENDING THE REST OF HIS DAYS WITH HIS NOSE UP A HORSE'S BUM!

If you think that's bad, you should meet Nebuchadnezzar. He can't sit down. Actually, it's not just sitting. He has trouble standing, squatting, lying, running, leaning, jumping, skipping, turning, sliding, hopping, pointing, smiling, winking, nudging, tapping, flicking and opening a can of beans. Just about the only thing he can do is DRIP.

THE KINGDOM OF WAX

Nebuchadnezzar was born on 25 December which meant that his parents got all excited and thought they were being rewarded for being such regular church-goers.

'Rewarded?' said the vicar. 'In what way?'

'Isn't it obvious?' said Nebuchadnezzar's mum. 'Our son was born on Christmas day, therefore he is very important.'

The churchman frowned.

'Oh come on, vicar, you know! He is more important than other kids, because he's a bit like *another* baby born on Christmas Day . . .'

The vicar spluttered into his cup of tea. 'You're not suggesting—'

'I'm not *suggesting* anything,' said Nebuchadnezzar's mum. 'I'm *saying* he's a bit like Jesus.'

'Are you serious?' gasped the vicar.

Nebuchadnezzar's parents, with their whiter-than-white lives, were always serious.

* * *

Because of the date of his birth, Nebuchadnezzar's parents had listened intently to every word that their son uttered. When he said, 'Googoo-gaga' or 'Nebuchadnezzar want potty' they wrote it down in a big black book so that future generations could study his words of wisdom. When he said, 'Can I have a tattoo like Trevor Pondlife?' he was locked into his bedroom and told to wear sandals. When his little sister's pets fell sick he was made to hold them in his healing hands until they were better. They all died, but he still had to do it. And while other children were playing football or flirting he was whisked off to church seven days a week so that he could learn all about his other father, God.

Every evening before supper Nebuchadnezzar's parents dressed him in his Sunday best, smoothed his hair down with palmfuls of spit until it lay flat like the slicked-down coat of an otter, and trotted off to the church for an hour of Bible readings and sermons. Afterwards they would descend into the church crypt, down amongst the stone tombs, where Nebuchadnezzar's parents had built a wax museum to the glory of God. It was called 'The Kingdom of Wax' and was an unusual place, to say the least.

They had made wax figures of all the modern

celebrities standing around in Biblical poses. So the Nativity scene in the barn had David and Victoria Beckham as Joseph and Mary, and Wayne Rooney providing the face for the baby Jesus. Adam and Eve were Peter Andre and Jordan, while alongside them in the jungle stood their troublesome sons, Cain and Abel, as depicted by the bald brothers, Phil and Grant Mitchell from *EastEnders*. Noah and his wife were Sir Steve Redgrave and Ellen Macarthur, and Moses, who was chosen to lead the Israelites into the Promised Land, was fleshed out by Jose Mourinho.

The idea behind the museum was to bring the Bible stories to the people, especially *young* people, and to make money for the church. Nebuchadnezzar found the place creepy, especially the figure of Jamie Oliver feeding the five thousand with a fish-gutting knife in his hand. His cold eyes followed Nebuchadnezzar wherever he went and convinced the boy that the waxworks were alive.

> Me! Me! Me! Me! Me! Me! Me!

That's just Sammy having problems brushing his teeth. These days he can't fit the brush in his mouth and keeps poking himself in the eye.

* * *

By the time Nebuchadnezzar was ten it was clear that he was not very good at being another Jesus. He was always clean and polite (as his parents demanded), but he wasn't a miracle-worker. He could only turn water into wine by adding blackcurrant juice and he couldn't walk on water to save his life. When he tried it at the local swimming pool, he sank to the bottom like a stone. From that day on the lifeguard insisted he wore armbands.

Then, forty days after his eleventh birthday, the neat and ordered life of this ordinary boy went into freefall. A 'Me!' Monster crawled under his skin and turned him sour.

It all started, because the headmistress made an announcement at Monday Assembly.

'On Friday night,' she informed her pupils, 'there is to be a Strictly Dance Fever Leavers' Ball for all Year Sevens.' There was a hum of excitement in the hall. 'Only this year, we are doing it a little differently,' she said. 'The girls will be choosing their partners, so it's up to the boys to impress them!'

It was as if somebody had flicked a switch in Nebuchadnezzar's brain. He had never thought about girls before, but now the prospect of being chosen by one, maybe even *touching* one, sent the Bible Boy into a hot mucky sweat. The hormones kicked in and by suppertime he was a different person. A rebel.

'I'm giving up church,' he announced to his mother and father. 'I have better things to do with my time than being godly.'

'This is the Devil talking,' said his mother in a whispering hiss that crackled with dread.

'No it's *me*,' said Nebuchadnezzar. 'I shall no longer be wearing my hair in a spit-down slick or my suit with three gold buttons. From now on, instead of devoting my life to being Jesus I shall devote my life to being attractive to girls!'

'I knew this would happen if we sent you to school!' she trembled.

'What's wrong with girls?' asked Nebuchadnezzar.

'Nothing,' shouted Ruth, his lippy little sister. 'We're made from honey and doughnuts and they are quite the most delicious things on the planet.'

'Be quiet!' boomed their father. 'Girls are temptation, Nebuchadnezzar! They will lead you from the path of righteousness and distract you from your purpose here on Earth.'

'Oh, my purpose here on Earth,' mocked the boy.

'Remind me what that is again.' Before the 'Me!' Monster arrived he would never have dared to speak to his father like that.

'To live a life of goodness,' came the thinly-controlled reply. 'To forego life's fatal fripperies such as vanity, money and fashion!'

'Resist temptation!' exclaimed his mother. 'Or pay the price! For where there is sin there is *always* a price to pay.'

I like to think there's a price to pay even if NO sin's been committed. Keeps it much fairer that way.

Nebuchadnezzar left his parents frothing in the kitchen and took his sister up to his bedroom for a secret word.

'Are we playing Hide and Hide?' she asked. 'Is that why we're *both* lying under your bed?'

'No,' he whispered. 'I don't want mum and dad to hear. The thing is, Ruth, I was wondering if you knew what girls like in a boy.'

'I do know,' she said proudly. 'Girls like the pointy end of a pencil in a boy. Or a compass. Both hurt.'

'No. What do girls find attractive in a boy?'

'Oh I see,' she said, 'What do girls *like* in a boy? Hmm. That's tricky. You want something that all girls like?'

'Yes.' Nebuchadnezzar was losing his patience.

'Apart from chocolate and baked beans, which, incidentally,' sniggered Ruth, 'make rude girls do windy-puffs.'

'Apart from those, yes.'

'Well, after long consideration, I think girls like a beautiful face, which, I have to say, *you* are going to struggle with, and a nice jacket with deep pockets that are always full of ice cream!'

Nebuchadnezzar was no nearer to discovering the Secret of Girl than he had been half an hour earlier. What he *did* discover when he woke up the following morning, however, was what girls *didn't* like. He was scraping the sleep from his eyes in the bathroom when he caught sight of his fringe. Normally, it was slick-spitted to his scalp, but on this particular morning it had sprung up like the bonnet of a car.

'Oh no,' he thought. 'Mother and father were right. I'm being punished for thinking about girls. My hair has sprung up to stop girls finding me attractive!'

His parents confirmed that this was indeed the situation. 'This is a punishment from on high for your godless behaviour,' said his father in a voice charged with disappointment.

'Chasing after girls and ignoring your devotions,' twitched his mother, 'is a deadly sin!'

* * *

It certainly *seemed* like a punishment when he walked into the playground later that day. The girls laughed heartlessly and cried, 'Bed-head, Bed-head, bet you wish that you were dead!'

Nebuchadnezzar had never felt less attractive to girls in his life. It did not escape his notice, however, that the boys who successfully caught girls' eyes all looked the same. They had fixed their hair into impossibly high hair-stacks, climbing six inches into the sky and sweeping forward like giant waves.

'What's your secret?' he asked a boy with his arms around three girls at the same time.

'Wax,' he slurred without moving his lips. 'Gel is hell, but wax is max.'

This presented Nebuchadnezzar with a problem. Up until now his parents had banned him from visiting such cesspits of immorality as chemists' and market stalls. Not only did he not know where to *find* this wax, but he had no money to buy it.

'Pocket money!' his father had shrieked two years earlier, when Nebuchadnezzar had asked him for some. 'Never! Look what happened to the prodigal son! Pocket money didn't do him any good, did it?' This meant that when Nebuchadnezzar finally found this wax it would have to be free. *Free wax* — where should he look for that?

* * *

Nine hours later, as the church clock struck midnight, Nebuchadnezzar slipped out of his bedroom into a starless night. There was a window at the back of the church that was always left open for stray cats. The vicar let them kip over in return for keeping down the rats in the crypt. As it happened this was where Nebuchadnezzar was headed when he squeezed through the gap between sill and frame and dropped into the vestry.

The Kingdom of Wax was in darkness as he tiptoed down the steps. The floor of the crypt flickered with shadows and somewhere, amplified by the stone walls, a slow trickle of water dripped into a tin bucket. Nebuchadnezzar switched on his torch and flashed it around the room. Hidden eyes sparkled in the dark as the light hit their glass pupils, then a flash from a fish-gutting knife and a glint from the polished apple in Eve's hand. Nebuchadnezzar was not planning to steal a whole body, just enough so that nobody would notice: an ear from The Good Samaritan; a nose from Judas Iscariot; some fingers or maybe a kneecap from the leper.

This was the beginning of the end.
In pursuit of self-worship.
Nebuchadnezzar had turned himself into a thief!

Back at home he placed the wax body parts in a casserole dish, put the casserole dish in the oven on a low heat, then went back to bed. Three hours later, he rose before anyone else was awake, took the casserole dish out of the oven and, using the side of the kettle as a styling mirror, worked the melted wax into his hair. He had to work quickly before the wax set, but after only a few minutes he had managed to stand his hair upright. Then he washed the casserole dish, put it back in the cupboard and went upstairs to get dressed.

'What have you done to yourself now!' wailed his mother when she caught sight of his hair at breakfast. He was trying to hide it behind a newspaper.

'Erm, It was like this when I woke up,' he said.

'Covered in wax!' she thundered. 'There is the

Devil in you, Nebuchadnezzar.'

'To be sure,' roared his father. 'You will fry in the flames of eternal damnation!'

On his way to school, Nebuchadnezzar was amused by his parents' reaction. It was obvious to him that what they'd said was nonsense. Nobody fried in the flames of eternal damnation for trying to look their best for girls! He wasn't so sure about stealing, though. He'd heard the Devil was quite a stickler on theft.

 Not wrong there!

'So don't get caught,' he told himself.

* * *

Of course the need for more wax could have been avoided had a girl come forward there and then to choose Nebuchadnezzar as her date. But none did. This was because the other boys had raised their game. Instead of just having big hair, they had opted for hair *sculptures* to lure the ladies. They had moulded their hair into unusual shapes; mopeds, toadstools and even a crouching squirrel. By comparison, Nebuchadnezzar's straight-up-and-down hair looked horribly old-fashioned, which was why, by the end of the day, he was still dateless.

So that night he stole a little bit more wax and hoped that nobody would notice. As he took a knife to Gary Lineker's ears, however, he heard a noise behind him.

'Who's there?' he called out. No reply came. Just a squelch and a soggy plop that sounded to Nebuchadnezzar like a wax foot separating from a stone floor and taking a pace towards him. He didn't wait to find out if he was right.

Back at home, the rest of the night followed a familiar pattern. He heated the wax in the casserole dish, went to sleep, woke up and moulded his hair into the shape of a horse's head. He had wanted to mould a lion's head, but the wax had set off before he could shorten the nose. Then he washed the pot, lied to his parents about waking up with his hair in this shape, ignored their cries of 'It'll all end in flames!' and rushed off to school to strut his fetlocks in front of the girls. Sadly, the horse impressed no-one and at the end of the day, he went home dateless again.

So that night he stole a little bit more wax and hoped that nobody would notice. He relieved JK Rowling of her hands, ran out before the spooky footsteps could catch him, melted the hands in the casserole dish, went to sleep, woke up, shaped his hair into a cheeseburger (because he'd noticed that girls liked cheeseburgers), washed the pot, lied to his parents and ran to school. He was *still* not chosen.

* * *

Come Thursday night he was desperate. There was only one day left to be picked and his chances were not looking good. The only girl who had still to choose her date was One-Toothed Tina and she was notorious for hating boys. Her passion was rugby, which was how she had lost her teeth. But Nebuchadnezzar's hormones were not choosy. If One-Toothed Tina could be persuaded to take him to the ball then he would go.

So he was careless. In his desperation, he took more wax than he needed. Not just Peter Andre's feet, but Sir Steve Redgrave's nose, Ellen Macarthur's smile and David Beckham's six-pack too. Then he ran in terror from the moving shadows, melted the wax in the casserole, went to sleep, woke up, sculpted his hair into an object that would attract One-Toothed Tina, and lied to his parents at the breakfast table.

'What's happened to your hair now?' they gawped.

'*The Lord moves in a mysterious way,*' said Nebuchadnezzar, '*his hairdos to perform.* I think you'll find that God has a secret desire to be a hairdresser and practises on people when they're asleep.'

'How dare you take his name in vain!' roared his mother. 'May you burn in Hell for that remark!'

'So you keep saying,' said Nebuchadnezzar, heading for the door, 'but I'm still here, aren't I?' Once out on the open pavement strong side winds buffeted his fifteen-foot hair-sculpture as he took a new route into school to avoid low bridges.

The waxed-up hair sculpture worked. Nebuchadnezzar finally got his girl, attracting One-Toothed Tina with his scaled down replica of Twickenham Rugby Stadium!

But that night, when Nebuchadnezzar should have been having the time of his life with Tina, his carelessness came home to roost. Just before he left for the ball, his parents staggered back from the church with pale and tortured faces.

'Somebody's broken into the crypt!' whispered his mother.

'And mutilated the waxworks!' his father wailed. 'Why would someone do such a thing?'

'Don't know,' said Nebuchadnezzar, sitting there

with a stadium on his head.

'And what are you wearing?' cried his father, spotting the waistband of Nebuchadnezzar's boxers peeping over the top of his jeans. 'That's rude.'

'I'm going to the Leavers' Ball,' he said.

'WHAT'S THIS?!' The sudden ferocity of his mother's voice stopped the kitchen clock.

'What's what?' asked Nebuchadnezzar innocently.

'This casserole dish on the cooker is full of wax!'

 Nebuchadnezzar froze. Tina's stadium had taken so long to construct that he'd forgotten to wash it up. Now he had not only been caught stealing, but *lying* too.

'Right!' that was his mother. 'Come with me!' Then with twice the strength of Samson she dragged him upstairs, ignored his cries of 'But I *will* go to the ball!', pulled him out of his jeans, forced him into his suit with the three gold buttons and plunged his head into a bath full of cold water. Her aim was to wash his hair and flatten the stadium, but Nebuchadnezzar had massaged in so much wax over the last week that every strand was water resistant.

'You'll go as you are!' she growled.

'Go where?' said Nebuchadnezzar. But he knew where his parents were taking him. He could tell from the direction the car took when they reversed into the road. He was being taken to church to repent his sins in front of God!

When Nebuchadnezzar entered the church it was as if he'd come with his own personal tornado. The doors slammed shut behind him and anything that wasn't nailed down was picked up by an invisible hand and hurled across the nave.

'What's happening?' cried Nebuchadnezzar's father, as hymn books swirled around his head.

'Our thieving son has woken the demons of Hell!' howled his mother. 'They have come to drag him down into the fiery pits.' Nebuchadnezzar was starting to believe her. The church stank of rotten eggs and the scorching wind had overturned the pews and torn off the sign on the door to the crypt **'CLOSED DUE TO VANDALISM'**.

'Is this magic?' cried Ruth, who had been forced to come along, because they didn't have a babysitter.

'*Black* magic!' screamed her father, gathering the girl into his arms. The iron bolt suddenly snapped back and the oak door crashed open, revealing the blackness of the crypt beyond; a blackness that echoed with vengeful howls and that familiar sound of wet clay slapped onto marble. With horror, the boy realised that it was sticky feet climbing the steps from the crypt. Now he was scared. What had he unleashed? He'd only stolen a little wax to get himself a girlfriend. He hadn't meant to do any harm.

That's what they all say — if only 'Mel' Monsters would realise that a little less haste means a little more life!

One by one, the waxwork dummies scraped their heavy limbs over the top step and fell out into the church. Like a chorus line of the living dead, celebrities without eyes, ears, noses, hands and feet stumbled across the pews, and wailed, 'Give us back our wax!'

All of a sudden, as if a confession might make things better, Nebuchadnezzar shouted, 'I didn't mean to lie! I only took it for my hair.' A zombified Jordan extended a fingerless hand and cried out for her eyes. 'Where's me peepers?!'

Nebuchadnezzar backed away as the Mitchell brothers pushed her aside and came after him for their ears, without which they looked like two boiled eggs.

'Stay away from me!' shouted Nebuchadnezzar.

He tripped on the altar step and fell onto his back, but still the figures came looking for revenge: David and Victoria Beckham, Wayne Rooney, Sir Steve Redgrave, Ellen Macarthur, and Jose Mourinho. It was a celebrity wax attack and there could only be one winner.

'Mother! Father!' cried Nebuchadnezzar. 'Save me!' But his parents were on their knees praying. He felt waxy fingers digging into his flesh and scrambled backwards until the altar table was pressing against his shoulder blades. The altar table, laid for Communion with its candle burning! The candle, made from wax! Wax, the main component of Nebuchadnezzar's hair, and of course ... firelighters!

There was a *woomph*, like the sound of petrol catching fire. As Nebuchadnezzar thrust the altar candle into the spud-like face of baby Jesus, Wayne Rooney's head ignited like an Olympic torch and set fire to all the other celebrities around him. They flared brightly, blazed briefly, then quickly melted away. Within seconds their wailing had been reduced to a tiny, bubbling gurgle as they liquefied into a deep pool of blood red wax.

'Phew!' said Ruth, jumping out of her father's arms and splashing around in the waxy puddle.

'That was close.'

* * *

It *was* close. *Too* close for Nebuchadnezzar's parents. They were so horrified at how close they had come to losing their son that they had a change of heart. They did not rebuild the Kingdom of Wax.

In fact they gave up God, stopped going to church and started a pot-holing school in Climping. As for Nebuchadnezzar, he was allowed to have as many girlfriends as he liked, but it wasn't quite as simple as that. Because the wax had waterproofed his hair, Nebuchadnezzar couldn't wash it, and because he couldn't wash his hair it stank like a pair of fast bowler's socks, and because his hair stank like a pair of fast bowler's socks girls avoided him like the plague.

It was ironic, therefore, that the one tweak he had made to his looks in order to make himself attractive to girls had ultimately repulsed them. It was even more ironic that, on his fourteenth birthday as he leaned forward to blow out the candles on his birthday cake, one of the flames should kiss his waxy fringe. It caught fire like a candle wick. He flared brightly, blazed briefly, then quickly melted away. In less than six seconds, Nebuchadnezzar had liquefied into a deep pool of blood red wax.

His mother and father had been wrong. It wasn't the flames of eternal damnation that consumed him, but a fire born of hormones and vanity, theft and deception and misapplied hair wax. And that, as they say, was that. Nebuchadnezzar was waxed for ever and ever. Amen.

Here endeth the lesson.

In fact, he dripped down between the floorboards of the church and came through the ceiling of our ballroom. I now use Nebuchadnezzar, and ALL the other children who OVER-WAX their silly hair as sealing wax for the thousands of letters that I send back to worried parents. Obviously I can't write a different letter to every parent or I'd lose quality torture-time, so I have carefully constructed this catch-all letter which covers everything I might want to say and everything they might want to hear.

THE HOTHELL DARKNESS

LOST PROPERTY OFFICE

DEAR GRIEVING/RELIEVED PARENTS,

MY DEEPEST CONDOLENCES/GREAT NEWS! YOUR LITTLE HORROR(S)/DARLING(S) IS/ARE NEVER COMING HOME/OUT OF YOUR HAIR FOREVER. HE/SHE/THEY IS/ARE MINE NOW/NOT YOUR RESPONSIBILITY ANYMORE AND IS/ARE DOING SOMETHING USEFUL/BEING PUNISHED FOR THE FIRST TIME IN THEIR PRETTY/POINTLESS LITTLE LIVES. FOR EXAMPLE, I AM DRESSING UP YOUR CHILD(REN)/BRAT(S) IN HIS/HER/THEIR SUNDAY BEST/CONCRETE OVERCOAT(S) AND TAKING HIM/HER/THEM TO CHURCH TO SING IN THE CHOIR/BURYING THEM IN THE PILLARS THAT HOLD UP THIS HOTHELL. YOU CAN BE PROUD OF HIS/HER/THEIR CONTRIBUTION TO OUR LITTLE COMMUNITY/BUILDING DOWN HERE. WITHOUT HIM/HER/THEM EVERYTHING WOULD FALL TO WRACK AND RUIN.

HAVE A NICE/MISERABLE DAY/NIGHT/REST OF YOUR LIFE.

SINCERELY YOURS,

The Night-flight Porter

THE HOTHELL DARKNESS.

Everyone has their use down here. Even B.S. Brogan. Don't forget to keep looking for him. Might he be in this sentence? Or this one? No? You're looking for a full stop, aren't you? What you don't know is that even when you become a full stop BITS keep growing — like hair and fingernails. Who knows what he could be by now? With the right lengthed pony tail, he could be disguised as a comma. Or with long clawlike fingernails what's to stop him from concealing himself as a question mark

Me! Me! Me! Me! Me! Me! Me!

WARNING!

THIS NEXT STORY MAY CONTAIN NUTS.

That is not to say that all the other stories don't contains nuts too. What else would you call STUPID CHILDREN who STILL behave badly when they KNOW what unspeakable horrors await them in The Darkness if they do!

Me! Me! Me! Me! Me! Me! Me!

ME! ME! ME! ME! ME! ME! ME! ME!

THE BLOOD DOCTOR

Her name was Georgina, but she preferred to be known as Gorgeous George. Like all 'Me!' Monsters looking beautiful was Gorgeous George's life.

> She was SO vain she should have been called Mimi! (Gettit?)

She was eleven years old and lived the life of a pageant queen. Her parents, Mr and Mrs Sutcliffe, had made the mistake of entering her for Barnsley's Cutest Kiddie Competition when she was three. From that day onwards Gorgeous George had displayed an unnatural obsession with how she looked. She entered beauty pageants the length and breadth of Yorkshire, from Tadcaster to Northallerton, from Pocklington to Goole, and – here's the strange bit – *never won*. In eight years of competition she had never lifted a trophy, which went some way to explaining why she was quite so bitter and twisted; if she couldn't win by fair means she had to win by *foul*.

Gorgeous George stopped at nothing to knock out her opponents. In the dressing room before a competition, she undermined the other girls' confidence with casual, passing remarks like, 'Oh dear, Chloë, when did you break your nose? I never noticed it was squashed before. Oh no! Have I just said something terrible?'

She cut up bathing costumes with pinking shears, blow-torched ball gowns and filled up bottles of fake tan with liquid boot polish. She swapped hair spray for fly spray, sawed through stiletto heels until they were sufficiently weakened to snap on stage, and soaked armpits of dresses with tap water to look like manly sweat patches. In Bridlington, she made Jemima, the hot favourite, cry just before she went on stage to meet the judges.

'Good luck,' she said.

'Thanks,' mumbled Jemima.

'Nervous?'

'A bit.'

'Do you know what I do every time I'm nervous?' said Gorgeous George, smiling in a saintly way. 'I look at this photograph.' And she thrust a piece of paper under the nervous girl's nose.

The effect was instantaneous. With a splutter and a howl Jemima burst into tears. When she walked out onto the stage her cheeks were red and her eyes were puffy. She was laughed at by the audience, received the first UNPLACED of her career and was traumatised for the next three weeks.

Gorgeous George left with a fifth place and a cold stone in her heart where her conscience had once been. When she got home her parents were waiting for her with grim faces.

'What's wrong?' she said. 'Aren't you going to ask me how I did?'

'We know how you did,' said her father. 'We have just received a phone call from Jemima's parents.'

'What did *they* want?' sneered Gorgeous George.

'They said you showed Jemima a photograph that made her lose the pageant,' said Mrs Sutcliffe. 'We'd like to see it.'

'It's only a picture of pretty little kittens!' protested Gorgeous George. 'Honestly, anyone would think I was a monster!'

'The photograph!' Her father held out his hand and Gorgeous George reluctantly passed it over. 'Just pretty little kittens,' he trembled. '*Just pretty little*

kittens! Pretty little kittens being beaten to death with a cricket bat!' His voice exploded in a peak of rage.

'How was I to know that cricket bats made her cry!' sniggered Gorgeous George, misjudging the severity of her parents' mood. Her mother clutched the arms of her chair until her knuckles turned white.

'A cricket bat!' she gasped. 'It's history repeating itself.'

'What are you talking about?' said Mr Sutcliffe.

'Has mummy lost her marbles?' sniggered Gorgeous George.

'Great Aunt Wilma!' explained her mother. '1931. The Miss Huddersfield competition.'

'Ah,' said Mr Sutcliffe. 'Great Aunt Wilma. The family skeleton . . .'

'Will someone tell me what you're talking about?' Gorgeous George was on tenterhooks to find out what this Great Aunt Wilma had done.

'It's bad blood,' hissed Mrs Sutcliffe.

'What is?' said her daughter. 'You're making no sense.'

'Your Great Aunt Wilma entered the Miss Huddersfield Beauty Contest in 1931. She reached the final with four other girls, but she'd gone as far as she could. She was not what you'd describe as a "good-looker". In fact, most people said she looked like a man, but that was just because she did six shifts a week down the coal mine.'

'And played front row for Wigan,' added Mr Sutcliffe.

'So why is it bad blood?' asked Gorgeous George. 'You said it was bad blood.'

'She knew she wasn't going to win,' said her mother, 'so she broke her opponents' legs with a cricket bat.'

'You don't think there's a link between Wilma's cricket bat and the bat in Georgina's photograph, do you?' surmised Mr Sutcliffe.

'I don't *think*, I *know*,' cried his wife. 'There's bad blood in this family. That's why Georgina's the way she is. That's why she always has to be the centre of attention.'

'Well, it sounds like a load of mumbo jumbo to me,' scoffed Gorgeous George.

'Does it?' snapped her mother. 'You won't be saying that after the Blood Doctor's been.'

Mr Sutcliffe gasped. 'Not the Blood Doctor!'

'It must be,' said his wife.

'Blood Doctor?' laughed Gorgeous George. 'Is

this you trying to scare me?'

'Bad blood,' mumbled her mother. 'It *has* to be changed!'

* * *

Mr Sutcliffe was not quite so sure that changing his daughter's blood was the answer. He wanted to give her another chance first. He talked to his wife who reluctantly agreed that if Gorgeous George improved her behaviour at the next pageant, then changing her blood would not be necessary. Gorgeous George thanked her father and promised in future to be kind, generous and good.

But words are cheap and sometimes promises are only made to be broken.

The next beauty pageant was in Grimsby and in her new-found spirit of friendship Gorgeous George went straight up to Jemima and gave her a kiss on her cheek.

'Hello, Jemima,' she said sweetly. 'Sorry about last time. I didn't mean to upset you.' Gorgeous George spotted Jemima's parents watching their conversation closely. She gave them a friendly wave before putting her arm around Jemima's shoulder and leading her away.

'You look *so* pretty today,' she said, then added by way of conversation. 'You know, I've never noticed it before, but you're the spitting image of your mother. You've got her eyes and teeth. Mind you, you've got a bit of your father in there as well—' a cruel flicker of her lips was all that signalled what was to come '— in your sideburns.' Jemima covered her cheeks, howled like an orphaned ewe, ran off into her parents' arms and never competed again.

* * *

That was enough for Mrs Sutcliffe. She phoned up NHS Direct (manned by experienced nurses from the National Hurt Service) explained what was wrong with her daughter and asked for the Blood Doctor. One hour later, a motorbike pulled up outside Gorgeous George's house. Over its rear wheel there was a white box marked with a red cross and the word BLOOD. The motorcyclist was a tiny gnome of a man. He removed his heavy helmet, jumped off the saddle onto the exhaust pipe stretched up and opened the box. Then he pulled out a white sheet, a soft bag glinting with steel instruments, a roll of rubber hosing, a black Gladstone bag and eight empty milk bottles in a convenient carry-all. He threw the sheet onto the ground first, then chucked the rest of his equipment into the sheet. He leaped down, gathered the four corners of the sheet over his shoulder and dragged his bundle up the garden path. He stopped outside the front door, climbed onto a plant pot and rang the bell.

After strapping Gorgeous George to a kitchen chair and draining an armful of blood into a milk bottle, the Blood Doctor made himself a glass of boiling water and topped it up with the girl's blood.

'Exquisite,' he said, sniffing the pink brew with his nose. Then he took a swig, swilled it around on his palate and knocked it back with a jerk of his neck. 'Mmmm, delicious. There can be no doubt,' he smiled. 'It's bad!'

'I knew it!' cried Mrs Sutcliffe.

'A change of blood will change the child,' added the doctor. 'We'll have that "Me!" Monster out of her in no time at all. There is just one problem,' he went on, ripping off the plaster that he'd stuck on George's mouth to stop her screaming. 'I'm afraid I'm a little short.'

'A *little* short!' jeered Gorgeous George, furious that her parents had let a stranger steal her blood. 'You're a *lot* short! What are you, two-feet-four?' But that wasn't what the miniature doctor meant.

'I am a little short of blood,' he said firmly. 'I had to see a family of anaemic vampires last night and they drank every last drop in the bank. I do have other stuff I can put into a child's veins to replace bad blood, but there's always the possibility of side effects. That's why the manual says we're only allowed to change a person's blood *three times* before we have to stop.'

Mr Sutcliffe was puzzled. 'What this "other stuff"?' he said. 'I thought human beings had to have blood inside them or they died.'

'Oh dear me, no,' smiled the Blood Doctor. 'That's very old fashioned. These days, human beings can live for years without blood so long as they've got something *liquid* in their veins. *Wetness* is the key. So what shall we try first?'

'Now, hang on a minute . . .' interrupted Gorgeous George. 'These are *my* veins you're planning to drain. I think you should be asking *me* what I want to put in them.' But Mrs Sutcliffe knew that if her daughter was allowed to choose her course of treatment, she would choose to send the doctor home and leave the bad blood exactly where it was.

'What do you have?' she asked the Blood Doctor. 'Don't look at the child. Talk to me.'

The Blood Doctor slid his Gladstone bag onto the kitchen table, stood on a chair and sprang the lock. He opened the bag to reveal four bottles, each containing a different coloured liquid. The one he picked out was blue.

'Anti-freeze,' he said. 'We replace her blood with anti-freeze, in exactly the same way as you'd drain and refill a car radiator.'

'I'm not having anti-freeze in my body!' objected the girl.

'Talk to *me*,' barked Mrs Sutcliffe. 'How will it change her?'

'Well, she won't get cold in the winter, and on dark, frosty mornings she'll start first time.'

'You mean she'll get out of bed when we call her?'

'Precisely,' said the Blood Doctor.

'And come down to breakfast without having to be asked ten times?'

'Absolutely,' he said.

'Sounds good,' said Mrs Sutcliffe.

'Don't I get a say in this?' grumbled Gorgeous George.

'No,' said her mother. 'You gave up your rights in your own blood the day you started behaving like a spoilt little madam.'

'But lying in bed till all hours is good for my skin,' argued the girl. 'Supermodels swear by sleep to make them more beautiful.'

'I'm sure they do, but you're *not* a supermodel,' said her mother sharply. 'You're just a superdaughter and you'll do as your supermother says.' She was all smiles as she turned back to the doctor. 'I'd like to see what else you've got before I make my decision,' she said. 'Ooh, isn't this exciting; choosing a new daughter!'

* * *

The next vein-filler that the Blood Doctor offered up was tomato ketchup.

'It's a good colour match,' he told them. 'And excellent if you're thinking of pursuing a career as an actress.'

Gorgeous George's eyes lit up. 'I *like* acting!' she said.

'Well, with this in your veins you can do all your own stunts, because if anything goes wrong and you accidentally cut off an arm or something, you'll only bleed tomato ketchup.'

'I want *that* one!' shouted Gorgeous George.

'Well, you can't have it,' said her mother. 'Actresses are just as vain as Beauty Queens. What else?'

'How about this?' said the doctor, producing a bottle of blue blood.

'Ooh, is that royal blood?' shrieked Gorgeous George. 'Bagsy I'm a princess!'

'Not quite,' said the diminutive doctor, removing the cork from the bottle and wincing as he took a sniff. 'It comes from an ugly blue whale.'

'Absolutely not!' shouted Gorgeous George. 'I can't stand fish!'

The doctor refrained from telling her that a whale was not a fish, but a mammal, and pushed on. 'I do have another vein-filler in blue,' he said, 'but it's still on the bike.'

'What is it?' asked Mrs Sutcliffe.

'Ink,' he said.

'Ink!' chuckled Mr Sutcliffe. 'What does that do?'

'It'll make her very clever,' said the doctor. 'Like a teacher or a writer.'

'Why?'

'Because it's ink that forms the letters that form the words on every piece of paper in the world. Ink writes *everything*, from the shortest shopping list to the longest philosophical essay.'

Mrs Sutcliffe was interested. 'We'll

try that!' she said. 'It'll make a nice change to have an intelligent daughter for once, instead of the vain, fingernail-painting airhead we've got now!'

* * *

The only issue with this particular transfusion was the method of delivery. Gorgeous George sat up on the kitchen table and screamed in horror when the Blood Doctor returned from his motorbike with his hands full of giant squid.

'Don't bring that thing anywhere near me!' yelled the girl. 'I told you, I hate fish.' This time he *did* correct her. 'It's not a fish, it's an invertebrate, and I take my orders from your mother. Hold still.' He attached the squid to her face so that its beak was up her nose and the tube leading to its ink sack was in her mouth. Then the squid sucked and pumped simultaneously until it had removed all her blood and replaced it with five and a half litres of ink.

I can see it now — a whole chain of blood replacement clinics up and down the land called SQUIDLY KIDDLIES!

The transformation in Gorgeous George was immediate and extraordinary. She stopped admiring herself in mirrors and devoted the next three days to writing a sixty-four page thesis on Malvolio's vanity in Shakespeare's *Twelfth Night*. On the down side, whilst reading Leo Tolstoy's *War and Peace* in bed, she paper-cut herself on one of the pages and bled blue ink all over her mother's clean sheets.

* * *

The next day, the Blood Doctor was summoned back to remove the ink and replace it with a liquid that would not stain Mrs Sutcliffe's soft furnishings. They chose milk, which went in easily enough, but started causing problems during netball. Jumping up and down, running, bouncing, twisting and turning, caused the milk to turn into cheese. Gorgeous George found herself so short of breath that she was taken home and put to bed. Within an hour, however, the house was overrun by mice lured up from the cellar by the overpowering waft of gorgonzola.

'We're not having this!' declared Mrs Sutcliffe as she jumped onto a chair and gathered up her skirts. 'Get me that Blood Doctor!'

So the Blood Doctor was summoned for the third and final time, and Mr Sutcliffe begged him to search every corner of his Gladstone bag to see if he had some blood.

'All this "other stuff" causes more problems than it's worth,' he explained.

'I could put her *old* blood back,' offered the tiny doctor.

'Her *bad* blood?' exclaimed Mrs Sutcliffe.

'Yes please!' cried Gorgeous George. 'I want to be a beauty queen again.'

'No!' said her mother. 'What else have you got?'

'Nothing,' said the doctor. 'I mean there's this, but I hesitate to suggest it.' He blushed as he pulled out a jar from the bottom of his bag. 'It's something my mother gave me when I left home.'

'It's pickled walnuts!' cried Mr Sutcliffe. 'I *love* pickled walnuts! Are they a favourite of yours?'

'No,' said the tiddly doctor, 'I can't stand them, but mummy swore they were magic walnuts and would make me grow.'

'And did they?'

'What do you think?' came the prickly reply.

'Sorry,' said Mr Sutcliffe, patting the doctor on his head. Then he bent down and peered closely through the glass. 'And you're sure they're walnuts?' he asked. 'I mean they're round and wrinkled like walnuts, but why are they pink?'

'Aren't we missing the point?' interrupted

Gorgeous George excitedly. 'Pickled walnuts are soaked in vinegar, right? And vinegar preserves the walnuts *exactly as they were* when they went in the jar? So if I was to have vinegar in my veins *I* would be preserved exactly as I am now.'

'Technically, yes.' The Blood Doctor hedged his bets. 'In practice, though, it's never been proven.' But Gorgeous George wasn't listening.

'If I was preserved the way I am now,' she squealed, 'I could enter Beauty Pageants *forever*, because with vinegar in my veins I'll never die.'

'Steady on, Georgina.'

'No, mummy. Don't you see? This is my chance to live my dream. If I enter that many pageants I've got to win *one*, haven't I? Do it!'

'Do what?' gasped her mother.

'I want what the pickled walnuts have got!' shrieked the girl. 'Fill me up with vinegar!'

'Wait a moment,' cautioned Mr Sutcliffe. 'We have to be careful, Georgina. This is our last chance. If the vinegar doesn't work, you'll be stuck with the consequences.'

'He's right,' said the doctor.

'But what's the alternative?' reasoned the girl. 'Leave me with

82

veins full of cheese? I'll be dead before you can say Stinking Bishop!'

'Oh dear,' said her mother. 'Now *she's* right.'

'Of course I'm right,' cried Gorgeous George. 'You've got rid of the bad blood already. I'm a *good* girl now. So preserve me as I am and we can live happily ever after.' Mr and Mrs Sutcliffe glanced across at each other, while the Blood Doctor shrugged.

'I'm willing to give it a go if you are,' he said. Then, after a nod from her parents, he stuck a needle into her arm, attached one end to the rubber hose and placed the other end of the hose in an empty milk bottle. 'Grab an arm each and squeeze the cheese!'

* * *

An hour later the transfusion was complete and Gorgeous George was put to bed to recover. Downstairs the Blood Doctor packed up his instruments and hurried to the front door.

'Good luck with the pageants,' he said stretching up to reach the door handle. 'You couldn't turn it for me, could you?'

But just as Mr Sutcliffe opened the door the doctor cried out, 'I've forgotten my jar of pickled

83

walnuts,' and turned back towards the kitchen.

Mr Sutcliffe blocked his way. 'I've looked and can't find them,' he said.

'But my *mother* gave them to me,' protested the smaller man.

'And you said you didn't like the taste,' argued Mr Sutcliffe, pushing the doctor through the front door with unseemly haste. 'If I find them, I'll send them on.'

And with that he slammed the door and took the jar of pickled walnuts out of his jacket pocket. Then he unscrewed the lid and popped one in his mouth. He had *always* loved pickled walnuts!

The texture of the nut was soft and meaty. He put it on his tongue and licked off the residue of the vinegar before slowly biting down on the squashy flesh and splitting the walnut in half. Just then he heard his wife scream. He took the stairs three at a time and burst into Gorgeous George's bedroom, where Mrs Sutcliffe was sitting by her daughter's bed.

'Look at her!' she wailed. 'Look what the vinegar has done to her!' Mr Sutcliffe choked on the remains of the walnut in his mouth. He coughed as it slipped down the wrong way and lodged in his lung.

The vinegar had pickled his daughter from the

inside out. The ascetic acid had dried out her bones and made them crumble. Without a skeleton, her body had simply collapsed in on itself like a deflating football. Her skin had shrunk to fit by gathering itself into folds. Small and round; no arms, no legs, no head, just wrinkles. Gorgeous George looked like a walnut.

It's safe to say that this was the end of her career as a pageant queen. because in the history of beauty contests a wrinkled nut has NEVER won a prize!

* * *

After five or ten minutes of getting used to their daughter's new look, Gorgeous George's parents declared themselves chuffed with the result. Now that their daughter had lost her beauty she no longer needed to be driven all over the county to beauty pageants, and they could put their feet up. That night, Mr Sutcliffe popped his daughter in the jar with the rest of the Blood Doctor's walnuts, placed the jar on a shelf in the larder and went to bed a happy man.

In the morning, however, he and his wife noticed something strange. The walnuts had moved. They had all lined up along the back edge of the jar like on-stage contestants at a beauty pageant.

'Is it possible that the other walnuts were pageant queens as well?' Mrs Sutcliffe asked. Remembering the walnut he had eaten the day before, her husband's face drained of colour.

'I hope not,' he said softly. He thought it had tasted of hairspray.

'That suggests,' she continued, 'that he's done this before. That the Blood Doctor hunts down "Me!" Monsters and tricks them into changing their blood for vinegar!'

Mr Sutcliffe mumbled something unintelligible, then rushed into the bathroom to be sick.

Two nights later there was a break-in at the Sutcliffe home. The only thing that was taken was the jar of pickled walnuts, and the only clue left behind as to whom the thief might be was a footprint in the flowerbed outside the cat flap. From the size of the shoe, the police were convinced that the intruder was a small child.

But some of us know differently . . . don't we?

86

What you don't know is that the
Blood Doctor works for me. That's
why Gorgeous George is down here
now with all her wrinkly friends! Oh
yes, he's pulled that 'these are
pickled walnuts from my mummy' scam a
hundred times before. You'd be amazed how
many children get themselves in a pickle once
they become obsessed with their appearance! Like
Mr Sutcliffe. I keep them all on the pickle shelf
in the hothell larder. They're not all walnuts.
There's Tomato Katchup who's a tomato. Brianston
Pickle who's a carrot and my particular favourite,
Picalilly, who's a cucumber. Lilly was a silly girl.
She plucked out all her eyebrows till she looked
like a fish.

e! Me! Me! Me! Me! Me! Me! Me! Me! Me!

ME! ME! ME! ME!
ME! ME! ME! ME!

PiCKLeD
WaLNutS

Me! Me! Me! Me! Me! Me! Me! Me!

ME! ME! ME! ME!
ME! ME! ME! ME!

Me! Me! Me! Me! Me! Me! Me!

Me! Me! Me! Me! Me! Me! Me!

Ribbet Ribbet! Splat!

That reminds me. Next up is a grizzly fairy tale, in which nobody lives happily ever after. So if you're sitting uncomfortably, I shall begin.

Me! Me! Me! Me! Me! Me! Me! Me! Me! Me!

88

THE UGLY PRINCE

Once upon a time in the Land of Illwindia there lived a butt-ugly prince called Spencer. He had a face that looked like it had been put together in a Kindergarten art class. His nose gave a fair imitation of a squashed yoghurt pot, his eyeballs bulged from their sockets like two empty egg shells, his ears looked like they had been hacked from a sponge – one was small, while the other was as huge as a dinner plate, his chin was a breeding ground for warts, his top lip was spotty and his forehead jutted out from underneath his hairline like Ayer's Rock.

He hadn't always been ugly. When he was born he was as beautiful as any newborn baby, but it was soon evident that he had a less than beautiful side to his nature. He threw his first rattle out of the pram when he was given his first rattle and threw his first tantrum when the nurse picked his first rattle up and gave it back. He wanted everything his own way and when he didn't get it, his little face flushed red like a small electric fire.

At six weeks old he had his parents, King Rolf and Queen Betty, twisted around his little finger. When he cried, they rushed forward with expensive offerings to soothe his ruffled feathers; hand-knitted socks, strawberries and ice cream, talking teddy bears, monogrammed dummies, old nannies, young nannies, a bouncy castle, cashmere baby-gros and a 3G mobile phone. But nothing ever calmed him down. Once he'd got what he'd been screaming for, he just broke it and wanted something else. He was a wilful child who thought that he was the centre of the Universe, that every object on Earth, every animal, vegetable and mineral, every person and every toy ever invented was his to own by right.

What nobody had told him was that the centre of the Universe is a big black hole!

If he'd been my child I'd have just said NO. Then if he had carried on demanding stuff I'd have given him a big, black, poisonous SCORPION and told him it was a Bicky-Peg!

Dignitaries from across the world were invited to

Prince Spencer's christening; including the king and queen of neighbouring Needabitofalegupland and their baby daughter Britney. The royal households had publicly agreed that when Prince Spencer and Princess Britney were old enough they should be married, thus uniting the peoples of their two small countries in wealth and prosperity. As it happened, Spencer and Britney were rather well matched. As royal children they both lived in palaces, they both ate off silver plates and drank from silver tippy-uppy cups, and when they didn't get what they wanted they both screamed until a nanny lost her head.

* * *

After the ceremony, Spencer and Britney's prams were parked next to each other in the throne room.

'So that they can get to know each other,' Queen Betty explained coyly to her guests. But when Spencer received six hundred and fourteen presents and Britney none, she opened her lungs and screamed. On this one occasion, she did *not* get what she wanted, which was 'everything that Spencer had.'

Instead, because he was the christening boy, Spencer

got *his* wish, which was to have Britney locked in the dungeon where she couldn't steal his gifts.

Not that Spencer wanted them. As each gift was presented to him a pattern swiftly emerged. He tore off the wrapping  paper, glanced at what was inside, screamed loudly, hurled the gift away, then held out his arms for the next present, tore off the wrapping paper, glanced at what was inside, screamed loudly, hurled the gift away . . . And so it went on, until Spencer's Fairy Godmother, a two-hundred year old white witch known as Lala Lala Lala La (she did a bit of opera singing in her spare time) stepped forward with her present.

'This gift is very special,' she said, fluttering her wings with excitement. 'Guard it with your life.' For the first time that afternoon Spencer stopped screaming and looked at the parcel on his lap. 'Ah, the power of Providence; already it flows through you,' she smiled, stroking the baby's brow, which for once was not scrunched in a frown. 'For five hundred years, young Spencer, this gift has been passed down from generation to generation. It is known as the Chalice of Candour, for he that owns it shall always know the truth. And to know the

truth is to know which path to take in
life. Let it guide you, godson mine. Listen
to its advice when you are faced with a
difficult decision, and one day this chalice will make
you the most powerful and prosperous man in the
world.' Her speech received warm applause from
King Rolf and Queen Betty who realised what a
generous gift she had just given to their child –
wisdom and success. But Spencer thought it was
boring and hurled the chalice out of his pram,
whereupon it hit a stone unicorn and smashed into
a hundred pieces.

The horrified audience fell silent as the large
ruby at the centre of the chalice's design clattered to
the floor and split in half. The only noise in the
throne room came from Prince Spencer as he
screamed for his next present. Lala Lala Lala La
leaned over the royal cot and exhaled a lungful of
stale air.

'What have you done?' she hissed. 'That chalice
was priceless!'

Spencer grabbed onto one of her wings, levered
himself out of his cot until his face was
touching hers, then deliberately *increased*
the volume of his scream to show her that
he didn't care.

'Say sorry,' she cried. 'Say "sorry", Spencer, and I will forgive you.'

But in answer to her plea, he tugged down sharply on her wing. His Fairy Godmother gasped as the bone snapped.

'Then I curse you!' she howled. 'From now until the day you say "sorry"! For every act of selfishness you inflict on others, for every tantrum you throw, for every toy that you break, you will become uglier.' And with that she was gone, flitting through a time portal to find herself a Fairy Goddoctor to set her wing in plaster.

And that is why Prince Spencer was butt-ugly. As he grew older his selfishness did not abate. With every toy that shattered on the nursery floor, with every kick he planted on his nanny's bottom, with every scream he unleashed in the king and queen's faces, he became just a little bit uglier. A wart for smashing the ambassador's platinum paperweight, a bent nose for stamping his feet at the wet weather, a scar for rubbing his caviar into the Duchess's hair, a spot for slashing Van Gogh's 'Sunflowers', and a lump for kicking a lady-in-waiting's lap dog over the roof of the indoor swimming pool.

* * *

Thirteen years after Lala Lala Lala La had placed her curse on Prince Spencer's head, his monstrous features were just about cooked. He was so ugly that he had to wear a paper bag in public so as not to frighten babies or turn water fountains to stone. At home, the royal dogs refused to wag their tails in front of him and at school, he was banned from the football team unless he played in goal; the opposition forwards only had to take one look at his face and they would run away and hide. Yet through all of this Prince Spencer remained cheerful, because he knew that when he was old enough he would marry the most beautiful girl in the world. Princess Britney.

Or so he thought.

This is just a silly old poem that I made up and carved into the skull of a griffin.

'Mel' Monster
I am a 'Mel' Monster.
Vain is my art!
I've eaten your liver
Next it's your heart!

* * *

Princess Britney had indeed grown up to be beautiful – on the *outside*, that is. On the inside she was as twisted as a hangman's noose. Like Spencer, she thought nothing of sneering at people who did not have her advantages or station in life, and if non-royals ever approached her for a chat she sprayed them with insecticide to keep them at bay. To celebrate her thirteenth birthday she had demanded a masked ball. Every Prince in Illwindia and Needabitofalegupland was invited, including Prince Spencer, who turned up expecting to be feted as Britney's boyfriend. He was stopped at the door by the bouncers and told to remove the paper bag from his head.

'No,' he said haughtily. 'It's my mask. Beside I'm marrying the birthday girl, so unless you don't want to have a head on your neck when you brush your teeth tonight, you'd better let me in!'

The paper bag stayed put until he met up with Britney and her princess friends, who were dancing around their diamond tiaras that they'd piled up in the middle of the dancefloor.

'Who are you?' said Britney rudely. 'That's a greengrocer's bag on your head. Are you some sort of talking fruit?'

'I'm not a talking fruit,' said Spencer.

'Are you a vegetable then?' she snorted. 'Because you don't look too clever!' Her royal friends laughed like over-bred chipmunks.

'I am neither,' said Spencer. 'I am your husband.' When this remark was greeted by more giggling he thought it was time to reveal his identity. There was an audible gasp on the dancefloor when his face came out of the bag. The shocked DJ ripped the needle across the vinyl and the music came to a sudden and violent halt.

In the silence that followed Princess Britney screamed, then said in a voice that reeked with contempt, 'I can't marry *you*! You're horrible! I'd rather marry the back end of a baboon. Replace your bag immediately!'

'But it's all been arranged,' protested Spencer.

'Then I shall un-arrange it,' she screeched. 'If I was to marry a freak like you, I would have to be dead. Even then I'd want at least six doctors to sign my Death Certificate so there weren't any doubts; like one of the doctors missing the fact that one sixteenth of my eye was still alive so that I could *see* you!' She grabbed the handbag off Princess Natalie's shoulder, clicked it open and filled the pockets with sick. Prince Spencer was lost for words. For the first time in his life, he couldn't have what he wanted.

'But you can't say that,' he stammered. 'The only thing that's kept me going through this ugly curse is the thought that one day the most beautiful girl in the world will be my wife.'

'And there's the problem,' sneered Princess Britney. '*I* look like a rose, whereas *you* look like the stuff they put around a rose's roots.'

'Horse manure!' hooted Princess Yasmin. 'Gee-Gee guano!'

'Look, you don't have to make up your mind now,' said Spencer.

'But I already *have*,' she whispered angrily. 'How shall I put this so you get the message? In my garden there is a broken bucket. All it wants is a bit of love and attention. But even *that bucket* couldn't love you, and it doesn't have eyes or feelings like I do! So unless you want me to use you for a game of Pin the Tail on the Piggy, put your face away and trot along back to your sty!'

Prince Spencer retreated from the masked ball with jeers of derision ringing in his ears. It was the most humiliating night of his life and he did not know how he would ever face another human being again. He had the mirrors removed from his bedroom and locked himself away for the next five years with only his black thoughts for company. He thought about nothing else but exacting his revenge on Britney. When pictures of her appeared in newspapers he cut them out and stuck them on his bedroom walls. After a year they turned yellow; after three they began to fade.

But Prince Spencer's memory *never* faded. His embarrassment was as vivid five years later as it had been on the night of the masked ball.

You're not starting to feel sorry for him, are you? DON'T! He brought it all on himself by breaking the Chalice of Candour and chucking his toys out the pram!

* * *

Then one day, just after Princess Britney had turned eighteen, Prince Spencer saw an announcement on the back page of *Practical Princess Monthly*. Next to a picture of Britney it said . . .

FESTIVAL OF FROGS

This coming Sunday at Havalot Castle,
the home of the King and Queen of
Needabitofalegupland,
Princess Britney will kiss all the frogs in
the garden and will marry the first one
that turns into a man.

In the interview that followed, Princess Britney explained . . .

'Everyone knows where the most handsome princes come from. I mean when have you ever seen a princess kiss a frog and it's not been a gorgeous, handsome hunk of a prince? Exactly. So the idea behind my Festival of Frogs is to gather loads of frogs in my garden so that I can kiss them all. Then the first one to turn into a prince will be my husband. I shall marry him. It's as simple as that.'

The interviewer then asked Princess Britney if she was not promised to Prince Spencer of Illwindia, according to a contract drawn up between their two countries eighteen years before. 'So what if I was?' the princess was quoted as saying. 'I'm not marrying him. He's ugly!'

The pain was still raw for Prince Spencer. His eyes smarted with tears as he read her cruel parting shot. But they were tears of joy. At last, he had a plan to exact his revenge!

* * *

First he paid a visit to Lala Lala Lala La, whom he hadn't seen since his christening. She was living in a Magic Wood, in a tree-house made entirely out of morning dew.

'Who are you?' she barked, rubbing her milky eyes.

'You won't remember me,' he said. 'I'm your Fairy Godson, Prince Spencer.'

She hissed like a rattle snake. 'Have you come to say sorry?'

'For what?' he said.

'For breaking the blessed Chalice of Candour!'

'I don't *do* sorry,' said Spencer rudely. 'I'm a prince.' An apology would be an admission that he was wrong and he was *never* wrong.

'I see the ugly curse worked then!' cackled his godmother as she slipped on a pair of bottle-thick spectacles.

'Yes,' he said coldly. 'Ha ha!'

'Would you like me to undo it?'

'No,' he said.

'NO!' squealed the old lady, 'but you're as ugly as a bag of frogs.'

'Funny you should say that,' said Prince Spencer, 'but that's exactly what I've come to see you about.'

The old lady was confused.

'I *want* to be ugly,' he explained. 'If you reverse your curse and make me beautiful again my revenge won't work!' He then went on to outline his plan. 'I need a magic potion to turn me into a frog.'

'Why would any man need that?' she asked.

'To trick a girl I used to love,' he said bitterly. 'When she kisses me as a frog and I turn back into a man, she will have to marry me. She's already promised. But when she sees it's me with my ugly face she will be miserable for the rest of her life!'

There it was. Prince Spencer's evil plan.

* * *

Unfortunately, being a Fairy Godmother is a job that comes with a lifetime of responsibilities. Despite loathing her godson, Lala Lala Lala La had no other choice but to gave him the magic potion.

'Take two spoonfuls twenty four hours before the

kiss,' she said. 'Now go away.' It took him three days to find his way out of the Magic Wood, by which time it was already Saturday. He didn't have time to go home, so took the potion where he stood. In the flash of a lizard's eye, he shrank to the size of a small green doughnut and hopped off down the road, following the road signs (so helpfully erected by the Automobile Association) to THE FESTIVAL OF FROGS.

There was no way of knowing how many princes were in the garden, but there were certainly a lot of frogs. When Prince Spencer hopped through a hole in the fence he was impressed at the trouble to which Princess Britney had gone to make the day special. Chefs were handing out mayfly and aphid canapés, waiters were uncorking bottles of chilled pond water, gardeners were trimming the grass with polished lawnmowers to give the frogs the best view of the princess, and a footman in a wig and white gloves was holding a soft, purple cushion on to which each frog was hopping to be kissed.

As Prince Spencer bounced across the lawn towards the Princess he only had one thought in his mind; the look on her face when she realised that she had been tricked! She'd never forgive him.

She'd live in abject misery for the rest of her life. And he didn't care. Revenge was all that mattered. Getting what he wanted. That look would be enough!

He caught her eye as he jumped through the grass. She was wiping her lips after another slimy kiss and pulling a face that barely disguised her disgust. He smiled to himself and plunged on.

But as he did so, a wind blew up suddenly behind him accompanied by a sound that reminded him of the clash and thunder of Turkish scimitars. By the time he glanced over his shoulder the lawnmower was already upon him. He tried to hop out of its way, but could only hop into the flashing blades, which slit him and sliced him and plopped him out the other end!

'What have you done?' screamed Princess Britney. 'You've chopped one of the frogs in half.'

'Sorry, ma'am,' cowered the gardener. 'Didn't see it.'

'What if that was the one?' she screamed, slapping the back of the old man's head. 'What if that was the man I was going to marry?'

'Sorry,' he muttered. 'Won't happen again, ma'am.'

'No, it won't,' she cried. 'Pick it up!' She grabbed

the gardener by his ear and marched him into the kitchen with the two sticky halves of the frog in his hands. Then, to teach the old fool a lesson, she made him put both halves in the blender, whisk them up and *drink* them. 'Every last drop,' she bellowed as the gardener gagged. 'Don't you dare leave a speck of that spawn!'

And that was the end of Prince Spencer, which rather neatly proves that you can't have everything you want even if you are an heir to the throne.

I keep Prince Spencer's memory alive by holding an Official Brown Paper Bag Day in The Darkness. At the start of the day I make all my guests ugly by feeding them lemons till their faces pucker up. Then I choose the ugliest child and he or she has to keep their face exactly like that for the rest of their life! And if they don't, it's into the in-sink-erator they go! (That's what happened to Brenda, actually.)

Unlike Prince Spencer, Princess Britney learned nothing. In the misguided belief that princesses always get what they want, she carried on staging THE FESTIVAL OF FROGS every year for sixty-six years and in all that time she kissed a million and one frogs but never found a husband.

Ironically, the only proposal of marriage that she was ever to receive in the whole of her life was that of Prince Spencer's at the Masked Ball. Maybe her miserable life would have been just that little bit happier had she accepted. Still . . . who cares? They were both ugly and both got exactly what they deserved. I tell her that every day.

Oh yes, Princess Britney's a guest here too the oldest BABY in the world! When she first came in on her eighty-fourth birthday. I put her in THE AGEING SUITE she didn't complain once. The beauty of The Ageing Suite is that the microclimate keeps her vital organs alive while her body gets older and wrinklier. And you know what that means . . . Now that she's two hundred and thirty she looks exactly like a FROG!

As that great French poet Simone de Citroën Deux Cheveux once wrote . . .

When a princess doth share her looks
With a warty, wet grenouille
'Tis mighty hard to find a prince
Who'll say; 'Will you marry me?'

How tragically true!

They all come to me in the end; from big-eyed
frogs to big-headed footballers. Before I show
you what I mean, read this little tale first. If you
don't I'll have to Brenda you!

A LITTLE TALE

In a scientific study, three bees from the same hive were asked if they were famous.

The first bee, a modest worker called Drone 996,425, said, 'No. I've never been famous. Too many bees do the same job as me.'

The second bee was a soldier called Ordinary Joe. 'I was famous briefly,' he said, 'when I killed a wasp in a dog fight. But people soon forgot my name, and before long I was just Ordinary Joe again.'

The third bee was a fat, pampered Queen called Elizabeth, who couldn't do anything for herself, having spent all of her life being looked after. 'Of course I'm famous,' she said, licking her hamster-like cheeks. 'I'm the most famous bee in the hive, everyone knows my name. Even after my death I expect my name to be remembered for all eternity!'

But when a hungry bear turned up and smashed the hive out of its tree, you can guess which bee it ate. Not the drone, because he wasn't even in the hive. He was out in the fields working. Not the soldier, because he was guarding the front door and the force of the bear's blow knocked him into the next field. It was the Queen, of course: the corpulent Queen,

Me! Me! Me! Me! Me! Me! Me! Me! Me! Me! Me

Me! Me! Me! Me! Me! Me! Me! Me! Me! Me!

wedged into the comb of the hive like a succulent prune in a thimble. Unable to do anything for herself, the Queen could only sit there and wait for the bear to spot her. And spot her it did. It couldn't very easily miss her at *her size*. Years of being waited upon had left her too fat to move. So she just sat there, while the bear's claw skewered her body and plucked her from the hive. Then it popped her in its mouth and squelched her like a sheep's eye.

Me! Me! Me! Me! Me! Me! Me! Me! Me! Me!

This little tale only goes to prove that you're never as big as you think you are. Out there somewhere, there is always something larger than you that doesn't think you're famous — like ME! ME! ME! ME! ME! ME! ME! ME! ME! ME! ME! ME! ME! ME! ME! ME! ME! ME! ME! for example!

ME! ME! ME! ME! ME! ME! ME! ME!

ME! ME! ME! ME!
ME! ME! ME! ME!

Me! Me! Me! Me! Me! Me! Me! Me!
Me! Me! Me! Me! Me!

Me! Me! Me! Me! Me! Me

Me! Me! Me! Me! Me! Me! Me!

ME! ME! ME! ME! ME! ME! ME! ME! ME! ME! ME! ME! ME!

BIG HEAD

It all started out of nothing. Sammy Slitherall was a squitty little creep who couldn't even get into the school football team who, when passing a famous football stadium one day, got lost inside a large crowd. One half was dressed in red, the other half in blue. It was the day of the big Cup Final between Shellsuit Millionaires and the Royal Bank of Brunei Wanderers. A large hand grabbed him while he was walking along, minding his own business, and dragged him into a dark doorway.

'Want to be a team mascot?' whispered a thick set man in a camel coat, who later turned out to be the manager of Shellsuit Millionaires.

'A team mascot!' gasped Sammy. 'Me?'

'Yes,' said the manager. 'Our regular mascot's called in sick and you're about his size.'

'Are you offering me his job?' said Sammy

'No,' said the manager. 'It's just for today.'

'All right,' said Sammy. 'How much?'

'Ten quid.'

'Done!'

Three minutes later, he was inside the stadium, dressed in an all–blue kit, standing on a red carpet, shaking the hand of the England captain. A close up of Sammy's face was not only displayed on the huge screen at one end of the stadium, but was also beamed around the world to forty million people.

He even met the Queen. 'Do you want to be a footballer?' she asked him.

'Not really,' said Sammy. 'I wouldn't mind their dosh, though!'

The truth was Sammy hated football, but the money and fast cars looked good.

* * *

That night, on his way home from the match, people started recognising him.

'Aren't you that famous mascot off the telly?' they shouted across the street. Small boys asked him to autograph their shirts and three girls approached Sammy with an unusual request.

'Do you want to go behind that tree for a snog?' they said.

At the time, Sammy didn't stop to ask why they wanted to snog him, but ten minutes later, after a granny in a wheelchair had stolen his shirt as a souvenir, it dawned on him what was happening. He had become a footballing celebrity! People had seen his face on the telly and now he was famous!

Only it wasn't *quite* as good as it sounds. The attention went to Sammy's head and made him big-headed.

* * *

At home in his bedroom he pretended there was a crowd of screaming girls camped outside his window to catch a glimpse of his naked torso. He imagined himself on the front page of the tabloids as the winner of *I'm a Celebrity, Get Me a Milkshake!* He dreamed of driving to school in a limousine, and buying a sweet shop on a beach in Barbados where he could take all his friends during lunch break. And he sat in front of his bedroom mirror for hours conducting imaginary television interviews with impossibly beautiful female presenters.

PRESENTER *(Fiona Bambieyes, for it is she)*: So you're a famous footballer?

SAMMY *(immodestly)*: Yeah, well you know, I was the Shellsuit Millionaires team mascot for the Cup Final.

FIONA *(fluttering her eyelashes to cover for the fact that*

she knows nothing about football): So you're good at football?

SAMMY *(avoiding tricky question)*: Good. Yes. Ish. I mean, what is good?

FIONA *(stroking Sammy's arm)*: Well, presumably you have talent?

SAMMY *(confident that he has the answer to impress her)*: I have talent in one area of the beautiful game that is often overlooked.

FIONA *(drooling ever so slightly with anticipation)*: And what's that?

SAMMY: Do you want to see how far I can spit?

FIONA: *(after a long pause during which she struggles not to kiss him)*: Oh yes!!!

Don't forget. It was Sammy's fantasy.

* * *

Within a few weeks of Sammy becoming famous, however, his happiness was compromised. He may have been a global superstar, but he was still only eleven, and in his piggy bank he had just sixty-seven pence. The most important thing about being a footballing celebrity is not how good you are at football, but how good you *look*, and Sammy's lack of funds was preventing him from looking anything other than 'Grade A Pants'. He needed cash for a makeover.

He turned, in the middle of the night, while both his parents were asleep, to the inside pocket of his father's jacket, to his father's pigskin wallet and the unbridled joy of his father's credit card. With it he was able to spend his way into a celebrity lifestyle, buying must-have items such as designer clothes for £1,000, a personal trainer for £5,000, a half-share in a race horse for £20,000, and a pet dog called Ivor for £6.50.

Ivor was a bulldog with breathing difficulties. He broke wind with every waddling step, and had a leaky tap in his nose, which dripped snot over the floor. It was slipping in a pool of this green gunk that first drew Mr Slitherall's attention to the dog, which in turn drew his attention to the question of where Sammy had got the money to pay for a dog, which in turn led to his discovery that his credit card was missing, which in turn led to this, 'You little thief!!! This will never happen again, do you hear me? This spending is stopping right now!' But Sammy the footballing celebrity was used to getting what he wanted and refused to do as he was told.

'You puny mortals don't understand us celebrities, Daddy. We're a better breed of human, on a par with the gods.'

His father felt his pulmonary artery constrict with stress. 'Name me one thing you've done that makes you special. You can't even kick a ball without falling over!' Insults no longer affected Sammy. Now that he was famous *everyone* took pot-shots at him. It was water off a duck's back. 'Yes, yes, yes. Of course you're jealous daddy. Of course you want what I've got, but you can't have it, because you're just ordinary.'

'You're stealing my money!' cried Mr Slitherall.

'And sounding like a Big Head,' chipped in Sammy's mother.

'I have to have these expensive things,' explained Sammy, 'because if I don't people will start thinking I'm not a celebrity.'

'But you're *not!*' exclaimed Mr Slitherall.

One thing celebrities cannot abide is the truth.

'If that's the case,' exploded Sammy in a froth of fury, 'then how do you explain *this*?' And he flourished a one year membership card to a Beauty Salon. 'If I'm not a footballing celebrity how did I get *this*!' His father caught his breath and staggered backwards into a chair.

Everyone knew that Beauty Salons only allowed men to join if they were footballers!

* * *

The following morning, Sammy took Ivor with him to the Tan2Liza Beauty Salon and told Liza to make him and his dog look identical. She began by engraving both of them with 'I Love Me' tattoos on their lower backs and arms. Then she moved on to haircuts, giving Sammy a blue streak down the middle of his hair and Ivor an identical marking down the centre of his back and tail. Then she filed and painted their toenails, plucked their eyebrows, moisturised their eyes with slices of cucumber and sprayed them all over with Orange Glow Instant Tan.

Finally Liza produced the strips of hot wax that she used to remove unwanted body hair. Ivor said 'no' to full-fur removal, but Sammy insisted that they should look like two peas in a pod. With two loud rips, a scream and a howl, the strips of hot wax were torn off the skin, leaving Sammy's body fashionably hairless, but poor, pink Ivor looking more wrinkled than a football sock and slightly colder than a plucked chicken. With a true dash of celebrity meanness, Sammy took one look at his newly uglified dog and threw him out of the limousine window.

'I'm bored with you now,' he yawned. 'Bye bye!'

In marked contrast to the dog, however, Sammy thought that *he* looked gorgeous – every inch a megastar. When he appeared that night wearing a sarong, his parents fell about laughing.

'You're wearing a dress!' his father roared. 'You look like a girl!'

'It's fashionable,' sneered Sammy.

'Yes,' said his mother, 'for girls!'

Sammy was incensed. 'You're so old-fashioned. Check out any page of *Ciao* magazine. It's the rage.'

'It's a complete waste of money,' said his father.

'It's not a waste. I'm a celebrity!'

'You're a Big Head!' corrected Mrs Slitherall.

'Look, fame doesn't come cheap,' shouted Sammy. 'There are bound to be running costs!'

'Well, not paid for by me,' smiled Mr Slitherall, with the ice-cold composure of someone who knew that he had won. Then he cut up his credit card and phoned Tan2Liza Beauty Salon to inform Liza that Sammy had purchased his membership fraudulently and that if she allowed him back through her doors he would get the police to lock her up until her tan had faded. Sammy's membership was cancelled immediately.

This left impoverished Sammy with a dilemma. Did he forget about being a celebrity and go back to looking normal again, or get a paper-round and use his wages to pay a *backstreet* Beauty Salon to do the work for a fraction of the price?

There was no contest.

* * *

The dingy backstreet smelled of decay. It was the sort of cobbled street where murders happen. Sammy had found the address of the cheap beauty salon in the phone book and was standing in front of a worm-eaten door peeling with green paint. A piece of curled wood had been screwed into the panel above the letterbox. On it was written:

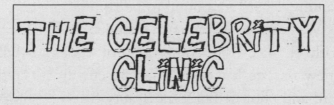

Then in teeny tiny letters underneath:

FOR BIG HEADS WHO WANT TO DROP A HAT SIZE

Unable to read the warning sign, Sammy stepped inside and found himself in a small room that smelled of joss-sticks. At one end there was a bamboo counter and, behind it, a red curtain separating the shop from a back room. The walls were covered from floor to ceiling in square drawers that had come from a Victorian chemist shop. On the floor burned an open fire. Smoke curled off the logs and licked around the base of an iron pot suspended in a three-legged cradle. Hanging down from the ceiling were herbs and dried flowers, the skeletons of birds and the white, leathery carcasses of salt-dried crocodiles. It was the strangest beauty salon Sammy had ever seen. Where were the tanning beds and nail bars?

'Hello!' he called out. There was a noise out the back, then the curtain was pulled across by an old man wearing a T-shirt and shorts. His skin was the colour of polished mahogany and his hair grew in short grey tufts. Around his neck was a garland of bright feathers. A toad was asleep on one of his shoulders, while on the other a baby crocodile, no bigger than a child's shoe, was hissing and spitting to scare Sammy off.

As he stepped into the shop and stroked his

unshaved chin, Sammy asked, 'Is this the Beauty Salon?'

'And who is you?' said the old man in a voice that sounded part-Australian.

'Sammy Slitherall. You probably recognise me off the telly.'

'No,' said the man. 'You want to know *my* name? It is Orang Kaya Pemancha of the Padeh, but you can call me Petebang for short.'

'Have you been in the beauty business long?' asked Sammy. He still wasn't sure if he was in the right place.

'Longtime,' said Petebang. 'First in Borneo and now here.'

'Oh, you're from Borneo?'

'From the Iban tribe. I'm shaman.'

'Oh, you're a shaman.' Sammy had heard of that word. 'Does that mean you do special head massages?'

'Sort of,' said Petebang. 'Shall we get on with it?' He pushed Sammy into a chair and stood directly behind him.

'What are you doing?' Sammy asked as Petebang ran his bony fingers through the boy's hair and probed the lines and contours of his skull.

'Got it!' he yelled. 'Here is the problem.'

'Problem?' laughed Sammy. 'I don't have a problem. I'm a celebrity. I'm perfect!'

The old man laughed like a crow. 'Not a bit of it. This is a serious case of celebrity-psychosis. The symptoms are most extreme and in need of urgent attention.' This was ridiculous. Sammy felt fine. 'What symptoms?' he asked.

'You have a severely swollen head and your ego is inflamed. I think also you may have ruptured your modesty, because I can't find it anywhere.'

'Now look here,' said Sammy. 'I came here for beauty treatment. We'll have a little less of the lecture, if you don't mind.'

'Where beauty is concerned,' said Petebang, 'there is only *inner* beauty. I deal in beauty of the soul, in returning people to balance with their life.'

'So you don't do manicures and mud packs?'

'You want a face pack?' The shaman chuckled darkly. 'OK!' Then he prepared a hot mustard face wrap to deal with Sammy's problem. It would sweat out the badness in Sammy's body and leave Sammy's face feeling tingly and fresh.

That wasn't all that it did!

Petebang wound the hot mustard bandages around Sammy's head until he looked like an Egyptian mummy. 'Now we wait for two hours,' he said.

'It's jolly hot!' mumbled Sammy.

'It'll be a lot hotter yet!' laughed the old man. 'The mustard sees to that!'

'Hang on!' Sammy shouted suddenly. 'I've just remembered what a shaman is – it's a witch doctor.' But he was shouting to himself, because Petebang had left the shop to take his crocodile for a walk. Sammy wanted to leave too, but he couldn't see a thing with the bandages on and he couldn't take the bandages off, because they were too hot to touch. So he sat where he was and waited for the shaman to return.

Sadly, it was the WAITING what did him in!

* * *

During the two hours that Petebang was away, the extreme heat inside the head wrap warmed up the hot air in Sammy's skull (of which there was rather a lot) until the pressure became so great that steam blasted out of his ears. This had the extraordinary effect of causing his head to deflate like a leaking football. When Petebang finally removed the bandages, Sammy's head was no bigger than a baby bee, which is generally accepted to be a slightly *less* than desirable size for a celebrity's head!

'What have you done to me?' squeaked Sammy.

'I've punctured your Big Head for ever!' roared the head-shrinking shaman from Borneo. 'Now nobody will want to know you!'

In fact, Petebang was wrong. With a head the size of a pea, Sammy *remained* famous, only now he was famous for all the wrong reasons.

'Ugh! Look!' kids jeered when he passed. 'It's Sammy Pin-Head!' Nobody wanted his autograph anymore. In fact nobody wanted the freak anywhere near them. They just wanted to run away from him as fast as they possibly could.

It's a lonely life being famous!

It's even lonelier in the Darkness. How did I get Sammy down here? Simple. I told him there was a supermarket to open and all the press would be here to meet him. He came gambolling down like a lamb to the slaughter! Now that I've got him, I keep him hanged up in the key cupboard behind reception. Then when guests lock themselves out of their rooms I use him as a skeleton key. There are two reasons for this.

1) His little head is just the right size to shove into a keyhole.

2) He's a skeleton since I forgot to feed him!

By the way, you haven't forgotten that the key to the front door is still in my underpants, have you? Crunch, crunch! Looks like you'll be staying after all. Under the circumstances, I'd be most obliged if you could take the time to fill out my Registration Form. If any  of the wording strikes you as sinister or odd that's because I have used different words to the ones that SHOULD be there. It's a sophisticated code which I use to defeat this ruthless gang of vagabonds who steal the words from Hothell Registration Forms, rearrange them into a different order, then use these rearranged words to say nasty things about me on the Internet!

I know! I can hardly believe it myself.

So please sign this form and don't ask any questions.

LAST WILL AND TESTAMENT

I . . . . BEING TERRIFIED OUT OF MY WITS
AND ONLY LITTLE DO HEREBY APPOINT THE NIGHT
NIGHT PORTER TO TAKE EVERYTHING I OWN AND BLOW
IT ON A 42-INCH HOME MOVIE SCREEN TO GO IN HIS
DEN. MORE IMPORTANTLY HE HAS MY PERMISSION TO
GO INTO MY HOUSE AT . . . . AND
TAKE ANYTHING HE FINDS THERE REGARDLESS OF
WHETHER IT BELONGS TO ME, AND IF HE'S HUNGRY, HE
CAN EAT MY RABBIT AND HAMSTER. I ALSO GIVE HIM
PERMISSION TO SNATCH ANY CHILD HE WANTS FROM
THEIR BED IN THE MIDDLE OF THEIR NIGHT WHETHER
THEY ARE AWAKE OR NOT, SO THAT HE CAN TURN
THEM INTO A FROG IN HIS AGEING ROOM OR IN-SINK-
ERATE THEM OR DO ANYTHING ELSE THAT IS NASTY TO
PAY THEM BACK FOR BEING EVIL LITTLE 'ME!'
MONSTERS! (EXCUSE THE CAPITAL LETTERS. GOT A BIT
CARRIED AWAY THERE.) NO POLICE CAN ARREST HIM
FOR ANY OF THIS, BECAUSE I SAID HE COULD DO IT
AND THIS IS MY LAST WILL AND TESTAMENT WHICH
MEANS THAT EVERYONE HAS TO DO WHAT I SAY IN
HERE. IT'S THE LAW.

SIGNED . . . .

All signed? Well done. Now close the book and let's
go find your room.

Freeze punk! My name is B.S. Brogan.
Are we at the end of the book yet?

Don't be so obvious. Brogan. Anyone can see
you're just trying to attach yourself to a
sentence at the end of the book so you can sneak
out under the back cover.

Is that what you think?

You can't get out. you crazy Full Stop. The
front door's locked and the key's in my underpants.

Recognise your friend?

'Me!' 'Me!' 'Me!' 'Me!' 'Me!' 'Me!' 'Me!' 'Me!'

No. Not Sammy! Put him back in the key cupboard.
His neck's not strong enough to open the front
door.

So are you going to stop me

Don't stick his head in the lock! I said. come back
here! You can't BOTH make a break for it!